FULL HOUSE

10 STORIES ABOUT POKER

FULL HOUSE

EDITED BY **PETE HAUTMAN**

G. P. PUTNAM'S SONS

G. P. PUTNAM'S SONS
A division of Penguin Young Readers Group.
Published by The Penguin Group.
Penguin Group (USA) Inc., 375 Hudson Street, New York, NY 10014, U.S.A.
Penguin Group (Canada), 90 Eglinton Avenue East, Suite 700, Toronto, Ontario, Canada M4P 2Y3
(a division of Pearson Penguin Canada Inc.).
Penguin Books Ltd, 80 Strand, London WC2R 0RL, England.
Penguin Ireland, 25 St. Stephen's Green, Dublin 2, Ireland (a division of Penguin Books Ltd.).
Penguin Group (Australia), 250 Camberwell Road, Camberwell, Victoria 3124, Australia
(a division of Pearson Australia Group Pty Ltd).
Penguin Books India Pvt Ltd, 11 Community Centre, Panchsheel Park, New Delhi—110 017, India.
Penguin Group (NZ), 67 Apollo Drive, Mairangi Bay, Auckland 1311, New Zealand
(a division of Pearson New Zealand Ltd.).
Penguin Books (South Africa) (Pty) Ltd, 24 Sturdee Avenue, Rosebank, Johannesburg 2196, South Africa.

Penguin Books Ltd, Registered Offices: 80 Strand, London WC2R 0RL, England.

Introduction copyright © 2007 by Pete Hautman.
"Poker for the Complete Idiot" copyright © 2007 by K. L. Going.
"Positively Cheat Street" copyright © 2007 by Francine Pascal.
"Dealing with the Devil" copyright © 2007 by Adam Stemple.
"The Cards That Are Hidden" copyright © 2007 by Alex Flinn.
"Sportin' Men" copyright © 2007 by Gary Phillips.
"The Royal Couple" copyright © 2007 by Mary Logue.
"Fiddy Dolla Smile" copyright © 2007 by Bill Fitzhugh.
"Suicide King" copyright © 2007 by Walter Sorrells.
"The Scholarship Game" copyright © 2007 by Pete Hautman.
"Up the River" copyright © 2007 by Will Weaver.

Published simultaneously in Canada. Printed in the United States of America.
Design by Katrina Damkoehler. Text set in Arrus.

Library of Congress Cataloging-in-Publication Data
Full house / edited by Pete Hautman.   p. cm.
1. Poker—Juvenile fiction. 2. Short stories, American. [1. Poker—Fiction. 2. Short stories.]
I. Hautman, Pete, 1952–   PZ5.P755 2007   [Fic]—dc22   2007014116

ISBN 978-0-399-24528-2
1   3   5   7   9   10   8   6   4   2
First Impression

CONTENTS

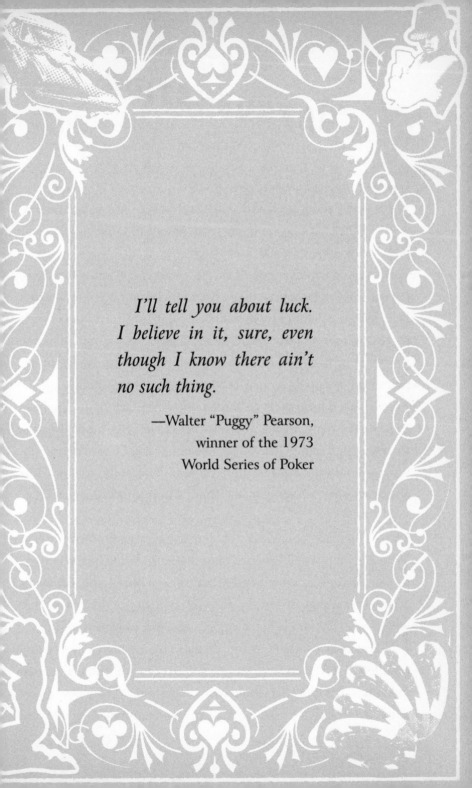

I'll tell you about luck. I believe in it, sure, even though I know there ain't no such thing.

—Walter "Puggy" Pearson,
winner of the 1973
World Series of Poker

INTRODUCTION

Is poker a game of luck, or a game of skill?

I learned about luck and skill—and poker—in the backseat of a 1957 Buick. At that time, the great American game of poker was only about 100 years old. I was eight.

The game was five-card draw, penny ante. You could bet up to ten cents. My teachers were my friend Ricky and his older brother Dan. We were on our way to their lake cabin for the weekend. Their parents were in the front seat, happy that we were not demanding ice cream or restroom stops. I had two dollars and change in my pocket for essentials such as candy, soda, and baseball cards.

We played for the entire three-hour drive. Dan dominated the game, betting and raising with ten-year-old ferocity. I quickly came to understand that poker was a game unlike any I had ever encountered—more exciting and more painful. This game was not just about winning or losing; it was about winning or losing *something*.

Thirty years later at a writers' conference, I learned something else: Writers love poker. I've since played poker with mystery writers, romance writers, sci-fi writers, writers of teen books, and just about every other variety of writer you could name. It occurred to me that writers who like to play poker might also like to write about it.

I also noticed that, in my many visits to high schools and middle schools, teens had embraced poker in a big way. Televised poker has introduced a whole new generation to the game. Poker chips in school have become nearly as common as iPods and backpacks. The famous poker legends—Doyle Brunson, Amarillo Slim, Stuey Ungar—are now as familiar to many teens as Tiger Woods, Shaquille O'Neal, or Tony Hawk.

At the same time, the world's top poker players are getting younger every year. Every year we see more players make their first million before their twenty-fifth birthday. For a teen with card smarts and a penchant for taking risks, the lure of big money poker can be irresistible.

Like most sports, poker has the potential to be both rewarding and dangerous, educational and mind-numbing, fulfilling and soul-shattering. The stories in this book explore the many guises of this great American game: weapon of vengeance, instrument of self-destruction, key to sudden wealth, ticket to love. Each writer brings his or her own unexpected and unique perspective, reminding us that every poker game is different—and the same. The players, the stakes, and even the rules change from one game to the next. But always—*always*—you can count on one thing: The cards will surprise you.

And so will these stories.

By the way, my first poker lesson? It ended shortly before we reached the lake cabin. Danny had won all my money. That was my first clue that poker was a game of skill. We played again the next day, after I found a dollar bill tucked into a secret compartment in my wallet. On the first hand I drew four cards to an ace and made a full house, winning two dollars. I understood then that poker was also a game of luck.

The combination of those two elemental forces—luck and skill—proved irresistible. I haven't passed up a game since.

Pete Hautman

THE RANKING OF POKER HANDS

All poker hands are composed of five cards. Higher ranked cards beat lower ranked cards (i.e., a queen beats a jack) except in high-low games, in which the highest hand and the lowest hand split the pot. Here are the nine possible poker hand combinations, ranked from highest to lowest.

Straight flush—Five sequential cards of the same suit. (A royal flush is an ace-high straight flush.)

Four-of-a-kind—Four cards of the same rank, with any fifth card.

Full house—Three-of-a-kind and a pair in the same hand.

Flush—Five cards of the same suit.

Straight—Five cards in sequence. (Aces can be used for high or low.)

Three-of-a-kind—Three cards of the same rank, with any two other cards.

Two pair—Two pairs, with any fifth card.

Pair—Two identically ranked cards, with any other three cards.

High card—When there are no pairs or better hands, the hand holding the highest cards wins. (A-K-6-4-2 beats A-Q-8-7-2.)

POKER FOR THE COMPLETE IDIOT

by K. L. Going

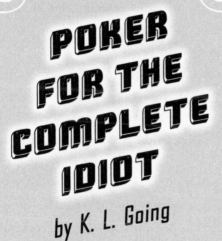

"Close your eyes."

Why would anyone close their eyes when Joanna Fox was leaning over their desk with her shirt open just enough to reveal some cleavage?

Fortunately for me, Joanna was doing it on purpose. I could tell because her eyes twinkled. There's nothing in the world as beautiful as Joanna Fox's eyes when they light up. Usually it happens when she's scheming something—like how to get me to wear a bright green cummerbund to the senior prom, or convincing me that double-dating with my little sister would be fun. But I love it anyway, and when Joanna twinkles like that, I end up doing whatever she asks.

So I closed my eyes.

"Stick out your hands," Joanna said, sexy as hell.

A couple X-rated thoughts raced through my brain, but I cleaned them up. After all, we were in school. Ninth period study hall. Mr. Thomas let us do what we wanted as long as no one got loud.

"What are you up to?" I asked, but Joanna just giggled.

I stuck out my hands, palms up, and felt a square box land on them. It was obviously a present—I could feel the foil wrapping paper and the string she'd used as a ribbon. It was not too heavy, but when I shook it there was a muffled sound.

"Open your eyes!"

I opened them and Joanna beamed. She bounced a couple times the way she did when she got real excited, but I was starting to sweat. Was it our anniversary? The day we first kissed? The day I asked her out for the second time—the time she actually said yes?

I tried to visualize the daily planner on my desk at home. I write everything on there. College application due dates. Birthdays. Appointments. *Anniversaries.* Then I tried to visualize the contents of my locker. Was there anything—*anything*—I could use as an emergency gift if I'd forgotten some big occasion?

"Open it, silly," Joanna said in her heaviest Tennessee accent.

My mind was jolted back to the box.

I kept that smile plastered on my face and tore open the red wrapping paper. *Please don't let it say Happy Anniversary*. When the paper was off I stared at the box in my hands. Inside was a trucker's cap emblazoned with the words *Card Shark*.

A strange gift considering I don't play cards.

"This is . . . great," I said, and Joanna bounced again.

"It's for poker night!" she sang, clapping her hands. "Daddy is inviting you to play with them this Saturday! Isn't that awesome?"

My first reaction was a rush of relief. Poker night—not an anniversary. I was safe. I let out a long breath and smiled for real, only it didn't last long. *What was I thinking?* Poker night with Joanna's father and two older brothers was about as far from safe as I could get. Ever heard of that comedian Jeff Foxworthy who does all the redneck jokes? *You know you're a redneck if . . . ?* Well, Joanna's family fits into every single joke and I was pretty sure boyfriend hunting was a pro sport for guys like that.

The Fox family probably has plenty of guns, too. They live in the most beat-up trailer park in all of Tennessee, and there are so many cars out front you'd think it was an auto shop. They've even got a pit bull. Plus, when Joanna's home they call her Jo-Jo. Oh, and did I mention her dad and brothers have hundreds of tattoos? They're like walking beef slabs with decorated biceps.

So, being invited to poker night was definitely *not* what I would consider awesome.

"They're inviting me?" I asked. "Why?"

I tried to say it without making the type of face you might make if your dentist told you it was time for a root canal, but Joanna cocked her head to one side and her eyes stopped twinkling.

"Dale, you've hardly spent any time with my family. You only say hi and bye to Daddy when you're picking me up, and don't think I haven't noticed how you're always late. You're ten minutes early to everything else, but when you've got to come by my place . . ."

"That's not true," I said, even though it was. Sometimes I even circled the park just to avoid being early.

"You only met Frankie and Warren once. They want to get to know you."

Yeah right. Guys like that didn't get to know anyone. And how exactly would we get acquainted? Talk about which college applications we'd completed or how to tell a carburetor from a spark plug?

"I told them how serious we've been getting lately," Joanna was saying, "and it was Daddy's suggestion to—"

"You told them what?!"

My stomach sank into my shoes.

"We are, aren't we?"

"Of course," I said, backtracking quickly. "I *do* want to spend time with your family. It's just . . ."

"Dale," Joanna said, interrupting, "it's a huge deal that they invited you. Daddy always said no Yankee could hold his own when it comes to poker, but I told him how smart you are. I told them you're the best guy I ever went out with."

My heart was somewhere between my stomach and my throat.

What could I say?

"You can play, can't you?" she asked, real quiet, the way a girl might ask if you liked her or not. "You told me you played poker," she added. "Remember?"

It's true. I had said that. Once. Before we were dating. When I was trying to convince her I was cool. And maybe I have played at some point in my life. I've played cards at least. Rummy, I think.

I stared at the hat.

A thousand thoughts went through my head. I thought about saying No, I can't play. I've never played. Joanna would be pissed, but only for a minute and then we'd laugh about it and she'd go home and tell her dad and brothers how lame I am. I thought about every sitcom where the entire plot hinged on one avoidable lie.

But then I thought one more thing.

It's a card game. If Joanna's redneck family can play it, how hard can it be?

Poker for the Complete Idiot.

I bought the book at the bookshop in town. It was Thursday and I had until Saturday. Plenty of time. Only, Thursday night was the track meet against Lexington County, so I didn't get home until late. Friday, I brought the book with me to school, but I didn't get to read it because the only free period I have is my ninth period study hall and guess who was being extra attentive?

Friday night I meant to read it, but Joanna practically insisted we go to the movies and since I was definitely on the "in" list at the moment I could tell there would be plenty of making out in the back of the theater. Between a book with "Idiot" in the title and a chance to reach under a beautiful girl's shirt in the dark, it wasn't a hard choice.

I wasn't even that worried. Near as I could tell, poker is a game of skill and strategy, and I was willing to bet I could hold my own with three auto mechanics and a pit bull in a trailer park.

So it was Saturday afternoon before I finally took out the book. It was larger than it looked in the store. I flipped through the table of contents, and there were sections on basic rules and strategies, all the different types of poker games, Internet poker, playing in casinos, entering tournaments, how to find funds . . . Funds were not a problem. I could take money out of my savings account with my ATM card before heading over to Joanna's, and I certainly didn't plan on playing in any tournaments or casinos, so the way I saw it, this was a good sign. I could skip three quarters of the book and not miss anything important.

I turned to the chapter on basic rules and definitions.

"Poker is a game about people and incomplete information. You not only play the odds, you also play the crowd . . ."

Yeah, yeah, yeah. I flipped ahead to the part about how to play the different types of games. I was ninety-nine percent sure Joanna had said her family played Texas Holdem, so I turned to that section and read it. I familiarized myself with phrases like "limping in" and "fit or fold." Good for impressing the guys. Then I glanced over the hand chart and dealt myself a couple sample rounds. Easy. The way I figured things, I was more than equipped to bluff my way through a couple hands of a card game.

Hickville, I thought, *here I come.*

That evening I arrived five minutes early just to make a point, and it was a good thing because it takes that long to navigate all the lawn ornaments.

The dog started barking as soon as I stepped onto the stairs, and Joanna and her mom came outside pretty fast. I could tell they were on their way to the mall. Joanna stood across from me on the top step while her mom went to start the car. She was wearing the soft blue sweater I jokingly called her security sweater. It picked up the color of her eyes and reminded me why I was about to waste an evening playing cards with hillbillies.

"Did you bring the hat I gave you?" she asked.

I pulled it out from inside my jacket and put it on.

"I come prepared," I joked, but she only grinned for a second.

"Dale," she told me, "don't try to . . . I mean, just be . . ."

I put my hand on her shoulder. She was probably worried about how her dad and brothers would act, and I wanted to let her know I could hold my own. When all was said and done, I wouldn't judge her because of her Neanderthal family.

"Relax," I said. "I can handle this."

"It's just . . ."

The horn beeped and Joanna searched out the car in the sea of automobiles littering her front yard. She spotted it, then turned back and kissed me on the cheek.

"Good luck tonight," she said, then just like that she was gone. I watched until the car sputtered out of sight and then I turned and rang the bell. It didn't work, so I had to pound on the door. I was wearing the hat and a long-sleeved plaid shirt, which was as close as I could come to country getup. The shirt got a smudge of grease on it straight off, but I figured that could only be a good thing, right?

It was Frankie who answered the door. He was three years

older than Joanna so he'd been a senior the year we were freshmen. At least, he should have been a senior. Frankie dropped out
the day he turned sixteen. Guess it would have been too embar-
rassing to be a freshman with a parking sticker.

He grinned when he saw me and I wondered what he
was thinking.

Let the games begin?

"Come on in," Frankie said, holding Brute the pit bull back by
a thread of a leash.

I edged through the front door.

"Hey, Dale. Good to see you." Joanna's Dad was standing in
the kitchen. I noticed the round table that was usually cluttered
with stuff had been cleared off and set up with cards and chips
and three cans of beer. One Coke. He walked across the kitchen
and shook my hand. His grip was so hard I couldn't help thinking
about The Rock in all those action flicks. He glanced at my cap,
but only for a second.

"Jo-Jo tells us you play some poker."

He said it like it was a fact, but I suspected it was a challenge.
I remembered a couple lines from my poker guide. Assess your
opponents. Never let them see you sweat. Actually, now that I
thought about it, the second one might have been from a com-
mercial or something. I couldn't quite remember, but I knew it
was time to bluff.

"Yes, sir," I said, "my family loves to play cards. My father is
quite a fan of the Six-Card Stud style."

I'd glanced through a section on varieties of poker and this
one seemed like a sure bet to impress. Then I wondered . . . was

it six or seven? I waited for Joanna's Dad to laugh, but he nodded real slowly.

"Is that right?" he asked.

I nodded back. That was a close call, but I guess I got it correct.

Just then Warren came in from outside. The door slammed shut and he sauntered in wearing one of those greasy T-shirts with no sleeves and torn jeans with cowboy boots. He took one look at my outfit and whistled through his teeth.

"You got to be kid—" he started, but Joanna's Dad cut him off.

"I think we're about ready to play, boys, wouldn't you say?"

Warren snorted and wiped his hands on his jeans.

"So," he said to me, "you're a card shark, huh?"

He had a mustache and biceps like a boxer. Despite the grease on my sleeve I was feeling pretty clean-cut and scrawny. I started to answer, but Warren didn't wait.

"Jo-Jo says you're pretty smart," he continued, slinging his legs over a kitchen chair. He glanced up at Joanna's Dad and they exchanged a look that probably meant, *We'll see about that.*

Joanna's Dad sat down across from us and cut the deck.

"You in, Frankie?" he asked. Frankie wasn't as big as Warren but he looked tough anyway. Maybe it was the way he guzzled his first beer without taking a breath.

"I'm in," he said, slamming down the beer can and glancing over at me. Something about that look made me think the phrase meant something else. Something about slaughtering the boy-friend, maybe? Some country ritual of humiliation?

"Nice hat," Frankie said, nodding at my trucker's cap.

"Thanks," I said. "I always wear it. It's like a good luck charm."

I thought that was a nice touch. Card players were superstitious, right?

Frankie laughed and Warren snorted, "I thought Jo-Jo just bought you that hat."

"Nah," I lied, blushing. "Different one."

Joanna's Dad cleared his throat.

"What are we playing?" he asked.

"Texas Holdem," I suggested, praying they'd agree since it was the only style I'd read about. "No limit," I added.

"Good choice," he said, raising one eyebrow. "Wouldn't you say, boys? Nice choice?"

Frankie and Warren nodded a little too fast.

As Joanna's Dad shuffled the cards, I reviewed everything in my mind. Full house was the best, right? One of everything? Or wait, was it five of a kind? High cards beat low cards? I was choking under pressure and that was rare for me.

I pulled at my collar and undid the top button. The trailer was definitely too small for four beefy guys (well okay, three beefy guys and one string bean) crowded around a small table in a tiny kitchen. Plus, I wasn't getting the hazing yet, and that was making me more nervous than if they'd just come out with it.

Then I remembered something. *Bluffing.*

That had to be it. There was no way these guys were truly this civilized. They had to be pretending to be nice, the same way I was pretending to be a card shark. Then at the right moment, they'd show their true boyfriend-hating hands . . . well, I made up my mind right then that I was going to call their bluff. This was one Yankee who wasn't going to be tricked into trusting trailer park trash.

The buy-in was one hundred dollars, and I was lucky I'd brought that much with me. I'd never even heard of a buy-in, so I'd been counting on starting off small and winning money as I went along. Fortunately, I'd been generous to myself at the ATM earlier.

Joanna's Dad dealt the cards, and the four of us were summing each other up. *So this,* I thought, *is poker*.

First round I was dealt a king and a queen.

Great cards. Must have been beginner's luck.

I bet a ton straight off and everyone looked real surprised, like they hadn't guessed I had it in me, but I wanted to make an impression. The flop was an ace, and then two nines, so I was doing pretty good. Lots of high cards and a pair. I bet again and Joanna's Dad raised, but I wanted to show them who was boss, so I called "All-in" just like the book had said.

"All-in?" Frankie asked. "On the first round? You sure about that?"

I fixed my best poker face.

"I'm sure," I said.

Frankie, Warren, and Joanna's Dad looked at each other across the table, then one by one they folded. What a feeling of power! I laid down my cards real cocky and for a long moment everyone stared. I could see the surprise on their faces. Then they looked at one another, and there was something in their expressions I couldn't read.

"Bet you thought I couldn't play," I joked.

Frankie nodded and Warren laughed, but Joanna's Dad cleared his throat.

"This round goes to Dale," he said, real firm, like he wasn't going to let his sons give me any slack about it. He gathered up the cards and handed them to Warren to shuffle and deal.

"Where'd you learn to play like *that?*" Warren asked, chuckling.

I wasn't about to say *Poker for the Complete Idiot*. I thought of all the stereotypes southern people have about northern people, like we have no family traditions and don't know how to cook. Or play poker. I decided I'd shoot them down right then since I don't abide by that kind of ignorance.

"It's a family thing," I said, even though that was a flat-out lie.

Warren raised one eyebrow.

"Huh," he said, but that was it.

Next round I folded, then the third round I folded again. Folding seemed like the perfect way to get through the night, but sooner or later I knew I'd have to bet again.

Finally, I got a queen and a ten. I tried to remember where they fit into that chart showing all the hand values. I thought they were somewhere in the middle, so I decided to give them a try. The flop was two, seven, and eight so I called and then the next card was a four. Things weren't looking so hot, but I kept playing, hoping for something better. No luck. The river card was an ace, and I was playing against Frankie. He bet five dollars.

This was the moment of truth. I could call his bet or fold. I looked at my cards. I had five hearts, which was cool looking, but I remembered clearly that I needed to have five in a row for a winning hand.

"I fold," I said, thinking it was a perfect time to show off some good sportsmanship. I laid down my cards so Frankie could see what I'd had, and his eyes popped when he saw my cards. He looked real confused, so I stuck my hand out across the table.

"Nice . . . job," I said, real slow so he could grasp the concept of someone being a good loser. Frankie looked over at his father and Joanna's Dad shrugged and nodded, so finally he reached across the table and shook my hand.

"Yeah, uh . . . thanks," he said, letting go of my hand and scooping in the pot, but he sure didn't look like he got how I could be so gracious about getting beaten fair and square.

It was Warren's turn to deal again. He took the cards and shuffled real slow. He glanced around the table, then cleared his throat.

Here it comes, I thought.

"You know," Warren said, "Jo-Jo tells us you're not so . . . comfortable . . . with her southern roots."

I gulped. Joanna had *said* that? To her father and brothers? A flash of anger passed over me, but I didn't have time to think about it.

"That's not . . ." I started, but Warren held up one hand.

"It's all right," he said. "I ain't meanin' to call you out on it. I just want you to know that we're capable of being real respectful of people when we set our minds to it."

He glanced at Frankie and their eyes got that same gleam Joanna's always got when she knew something I didn't know. I swallowed hard.

"Jo-Jo is real special to us," Warren continued. "She deserves the best and we've always tried to give it to her. We may not be rich, but we're pretty darn proud of each other."

There was silence for a moment, then Warren shuffled again extra slow so each card rippled against the next. I was starting to sweat, but I was determined to keep my cool.

"That's, uh, great," I said as Warren finally dealt the cards. "I don't know what Joanna told you, but I don't have any problem with her being from Tennessee. This is a great state, and she's a great girl."

Joanna's Dad nodded. "She sure is," he said. "Jo-Jo deserves someone with integrity. Someone who knows who he is and where he stands in life."

I glanced at my hand, distracted. I was back on familiar territory now. What guy hadn't heard this lecture before? *This girl deserves a prince. Someone who will treat her right. I better not hurt her . . . etc. etc.* The truth was, I might be in high school, but I felt pretty certain I could give Joanna a better future than this.

I sat up straight and studied my cards. Frankie and Joanna's Dad folded right away, and I only had a ten and a four, but I decided to bet half my chips anyway just to make a point.

See? I'm in.

Warren studied his cards. I could tell he was my toughest opponent.

"You know," he said, calling my bet, "Frankie could've gone to college if he'd wanted to, but there's only enough money for one of us to go and we all knew from the start it would be Jo-Jo. She's a dang smart girl. Jo-Jo ain't nobody's fool. You understand?"

Warren slowly placed three cards on the table, faceup, side by side. Looking at them, the only thing I understood at that moment was that I had nothing!

"Yeah," I said, swallowing hard. "That's cool."

Despite my bad hand, I ended up calling Warren's bet. Then the turn card was a crappy two, so I still didn't have anything, but I decided to keep up my bluff in hopes that Warren would fold. I bet all my chips.

Warren studied me like he knew exactly what I was doing.

"We probably spoiled her a bit," he said, at last, "but that's the way it was going to be from the start. Right, Dad?"

Joanna's Dad grinned.

"Yeah," he said, "that's right."

I wondered what all this small talk was getting to. If they meant to scare me they sure weren't doing a good job of it. At the moment, the only thing that was scaring me was whether Warren would call my bluff and I'd be out of the game.

There was a long silence while he and I locked eyes. Something scampered over my foot under the table—probably a cockroach—and it was all I could do not to stand up and stomp on it, but I didn't. I held my ground.

"I fold," Warren said at last, still looking me straight in the eye. He tossed his cards down on the table, and I looked frantically before he scooped them up. Two jacks.

Relief flooded through me.

Thank God, I thought. My bluff worked. Then I thought, *Damn. It turns out I'm good at this game.*

I scooped Warren's chips into my pile and tried not to act too relieved. I knew I'd passed a line of some sort. I'd faced down each of Joanna's family members and shown them exactly who was boss.

From this point on, the rest of the night would be cake.

"How did it go?"

Joanna must have dialed the phone as soon as she walked in the door. I hadn't been home ten minutes when she called.

"Great," I said. "I told you I could hold my own."

I could hear her breath rushing out.

"You guys got along okay?"

"Sure," I said. "It was all very sportsmanlike." *Thanks to me,* I thought.

Joanna giggled with relief.

"You are the best, Dale. I asked Daddy how it went and he said it was one hell of a game."

"Yeah. I guess it was."

"So tell me about it. I want to hear every detail."

I thought over the whole evening. My victory was still fresh in my mind, and their money was fresh in my pocket. I planned on using it to buy something special for Joanna.

"Well, first round I had great high cards, and then the flop gave me a pair so I went all-in. I guess they could tell I had a great hand because everyone folded. Beginner's luck, I'm sure," I added modestly.

There was a long silence on the other end of the phone line.

"All-in?" she said at last. "On your first hand? If the pair was in the flop it belonged to everyone. You wouldn't have gone all-in on that."

My mind raced. I remembered the way I'd laid my cards down on the table. I'd been *sure* I had the winning hand. One hundred percent positive. And no one had corrected me.

"Guess I must have forgotten what my hand was," I said, shrugging it off. "Anyway, it was a good one and it beat everyone cold."

Joanna didn't say anything.

"Of course, I lost one round to Frankie," I added quick. "Man, that was a miserable hand. He had two aces, and I had five hearts, but not in a row, so I was shot. But you know what? I took the opportunity to model good sportsmanship, and I think he really appreciated that."

There was silence again—long drawn-out silence. What was the deal here? I wasn't supposed to win *or* lose? What was her problem?

"You had a flush."

"What?"

"Five hearts is a flush."

Now I was really sweating. I grabbed the poker book off my floor and madly flipped through the pages. Hand rankings . . . flush . . . any combination of five cards of the same suit . . . oh shit.

But how could that be? Frankie had shaken my hand afterward when I'd spoken to him real loud and slow like he was deaf.

"Dale, maybe I should go."

"No, wait," I said. "Don't hang up. I haven't told you about the best round. Those were just the warm-ups."

I could feel her slipping away and I hurried to say something. Anything.

"My favorite round was when it was me and Warren, and we were talking about you, how great you are . . ." *Actually, now that I thought about it Warren had done most of the talking.* "And I had nothing in my hand, but I was bluffing, see, and Warren had a great hand, but . . ."

My voice was fading even as I tried to keep talking.

Warren had a great hand.

Fragments of the evening were coming back to me. Pieces of information I hadn't thought about until just now.

Frankie could have gone to college if he'd wanted to, but there was only enough money for one.

We're capable of being real respectful of people when we set our minds to it.

Jo-Jo ain't nobody's fool.

Had I won the game but been outplayed?

"Listen," Joanna said, "I'm going to hang up."

"Jo-Jo, don't . . ."

There was a click and then a dial tone.

Jo-Jo. I thought about everything I'd ever said about her family, all the jokes she'd tried to laugh at. Then I heard her dad's voice in my head.

"She deserves someone with integrity. Someone who knows who he is and where he stands in life."

I picked up the poker book and stared at the words on the cover. Finally, I understood.

Poker for the Complete . . .

Idiot.

K. L. Going

K. L. Going is the award-winning author of books for children and teens. Her first novel, *Fat Kid Rules the World*, was named a Michael Printz Honor book by the American Library Association, as well as one of the Best Books for Young Adults from the past decade. Her second novel, *The Liberation of Gabriel King*, was chosen as a notable book by the International Reading Association and a Book Sense pick by independent booksellers. K. L.'s third novel, *Saint Iggy*, is also a Book Sense pick and was named as one of *Publishers Weekly*'s Best Books of 2006. She lives and writes full-time in Glen Spey, NY.

K. L. wishes she were a card shark, but unfortunately she's not. "I played my first hand of poker in a rest stop while traveling between New York and Maine just after I was asked to write this story. Even though I didn't know anything about poker, I thought I could use that to my advantage and craft a story around someone's lack of expertise rather than the more typical reverse scenario. I found out it takes a lot of knowledge to write about ignorance, but that's one of the things I love most about being an author. You get to learn all sorts of new things!"

POSITIVELY CHEAT STREET

by Francine Pascal

It's a totally guy game and they only
asked me because at the last minute they
lost their seventh player and I happen to
live next door so I guess they figured it
wouldn't be the end of the world if they
played with a girl this one time.

I'd met John, the guy whose apartment it was in, the week before in the
elevator, and since we both live on the
eighteenth floor there was plenty of time

to talk. Like too much. But he was cute and seventeen and I'm sixteen and new in New York and the building. Cute doesn't really do it, he was totally gorgeous, but kind of a little shy so it was heavy furniture making blah blah blah fill eighteen floors particularly since some butthead must have pushed all the buttons before he got off and we were stopping at practically every other floor.

We did the Where do you go to school? thing. He goes to Dalton on the east side and I go to Trinity on the west side. And then Where did I come from? LA, and How come I moved to New York? My dad is a writer and he got a sitcom that shoots here. By then we were only at the eleventh floor and still stopping and we were sort of out of stuff to talk about so he started in about his poker game and how he has a weekly game and somehow he got the impression that I was a good player.

He said, like, You play poker? And I said, I love poker. Technically I wasn't lying and if I had a little more time I would have told him about how when I was little after a family dinner this really nice uncle would get all the kids together on the floor and we would play poker with matchsticks and how much I loved it. But suddenly the elevator stopped, the doors opened and we were in the lobby and he was saying, See ya!

But I didn't see him until he rang my doorbell at about four in the afternoon two days later.

"Hey," he said.

You know how when a person is out of context, sort of not where he is supposed to be, for a minute you don't recognize him? It was only a nanosecond and then I did and I guess I smiled and he smiled and he has a slightly chipped front tooth that only makes him cuter. Date, I said to myself. He wants a date. I'll play it cool, I won't say yes until he asks me.

I was so busy concentrating on my cool that I didn't actually hear what he said, but I said yes anyway.

"The game starts at eight. You okay with that?"

"Game?" I said.

"Poker, remember, you said you loved it."

"Totally." And I closed the door fast before he could see the panic on my face.

Luckily, my dad plays poker so he has a lot of poker books around. And I'm a fast study.

I went through my dad's poker books, especially *McManus' Positively Fifth Street,* and memorized the what-beats-what stuff like it was for a test. Luckily, math is my best subject. I went through some of the hands and what's good and what's great and what's a loser and I was surprised at how much I remembered. That turned out to be the easy part.

The hard part?

What do you wear for a poker game?

Jeans. That's easy, but what top?

Everything's always about the tops. They've got to be sexy, but more like accidental sexy—after all, it's a poker game. That's sort of serious.

So now it's four fifteen; I can probably wait till four twenty to start working on the outfit. But maybe I should get a head start.

By five my room looks like someone threw up clothes. Even if most of my things weren't wrinkled from being rolled up and stuffed in my drawers I still probably have the way ugliest clothes in America. Where was I when I bought them? They must have had some magic mirrors in the stores. And the incredible thing is I haven't seen some of these things in years.

By seven thirty I have the perfect outfit. By twenty to eight I have an even more perfect outfit and by ten to eight, I find the totally perfect outfit. But I don't wear it because at the last minute I have an epiphany and go back to the first perfect outfit from four twenty.

I wait until ten after eight to ring John's doorbell. A tall, good-looking jock-type guy I don't know opens the door.

"Yeah?" Definitely not friendly.

"I'm here for the game."

And still not letting me in, he shouts back into the apartment, "Hey, John, you gotta be kidding."

And then John is there. "Don't be an asshole, Frank, let her in."

John's apartment faces Fifty-seventh Street and Seventh Avenue, and it's huge and all marble and glass and looks like something from a movie. Our whole apartment could fit in their front rooms and on top of that it's got these fabulous terraces. Obviously, he's way richer than we are and these guys are not going to be playing for matchsticks. Now I'm worried fifty dollars isn't going to be enough money. I have two hundred more in my desk from Christmas but I'm not ready to blow it on a poker game.

Even though Frank lets me in, he's blocking me like in a basketball game; I move this way and he's there, the other way, he's there. I'm barely here and already sorry I came.

"Hey, John," Frank says, and finally lets me by, "since when do you just invite anything around? If you wanted gash I coulda brought something we'd really want to play with."

That line is timed perfectly so that I just get to an open kitchen-family room with everyone at the poker table when he finishes so it's like my intro. They all turn to look at the gash, an expression I never heard but can figure out fast.

"Hi," I say, and John introduces me around. I already know and love Frank, and then there's Sam, an okay-looking guy who somewhere along the line took that extra Big Mac and never lost it. He grunts hi, and goes back to dividing the chips. Next to him is Noel. The only thing different about him is that he looks half Asian. Maybe not even half. It's hard to tell because he's got his head down counting out money and never looks up to say hello. Then comes Sean, a redhead whose face is all freckles; he's the first one to smile at me.

"Hey, welcome," he says.

Next to him is Jeff, a short skinny guy who turns out to be Sean's kid brother. I can tell Jeff is nervous, afraid if he says hello he'll be on the girl's team. Being a kid brother is hard enough.

Except for Jeff, who's about my age, they all look about eighteen or nineteen and if they have last names no one mentions them. And they all have bottles of Rolling Rock in front of them, including Jeff.

I say a general "hi" and take a seat next to Sean as far away from Frank as possible. John sits on the other side of me like he was protecting me, which is totally nice. He even gives me a beer. I actually don't much like beer, but I've got to look like one of the guys, so I say thanks and take a swallow.

I'm the last one to buy chips. It costs me thirty dollars, which leaves me a big twenty in my pocket. The whites are a dollar, the reds two dollars, and the blues are four.

The game is holdem high-low. Everyone gets two cards and the dealer puts five facedown in the middle. High hand and low hand split the pot. I studied this game the most and I feel okay about it but I never got to the part about the Rule of Eight so John explains it to me.

"To qualify for low," he says, "all five of your cards, the three on the table and the two in your hand, have to be eight or under."

Just to be sure I ask him to repeat it, but before he can, Frank says really nasty, "I thought you said she knew how to play."

John pays no attention to him and repeats the Rule of Eight, which isn't that difficult except I'm so nervous I can barely hear him. And sweaty. When Sean deals my fingers stick to the cards, but I'm happy with my seven and nine because according to the book I can go right out.

The first few hands are classic losers so I don't even wait for the flop.

"Is she ever gonna play?" Frank asks.

My next hand is about the best you can get for holdem, an ace and a king. Of course, I stay.

"Holy shit," my nemesis says, "she must have an ace and a king."

When two jacks come up and Sean starts raising, I go out. If it was Frank I would think he was bluffing to get me out, but Sean looks like he really has a jack. It costs me ten dollars. I'm going to need that Christmas money if I'm going to keep playing.

Then a weird thing happens. Maybe I'm the only one who sees it but Frank slides a couple of two-dollar chips out of the pot he didn't win and moves them in front of himself. Now they're his. He does it like he's helping the real winners, Jeff and John, split up the pot. I start watching him closely and more than once he goes light on his ante.

And then he does other things, like trying to peek at Noel or Jeff's cards, always little stuff, but absolutely cheating. And when he divides up the pot—he's always first to help—the other winners are sure to get stiffed.

I look around to see if anyone else notices, but they're all so busy talking or getting beers or whatever that they don't see what's going on. Only me.

And I think Frank knows that I see him cheat. The one time we share the pot he takes an extra few chips so fast it's like they were never there, and looks me dead in the eyes like he's saying, I dare you to say something.

And I don't.

After that one win I'm back to losers again. Nines seem to be my theme, so I excuse myself and slip back to my apartment to get more money. I figure I'll take fifty more but then I take the whole two hundred. I don't want to run out of cash in front of Frank.

On my way back to the table I run into Frank in the hallway. It's not a wide passage and he plays the basketball stuff again. This time, with his arms extended, he actually blocks me.

"Excuse me," I say and try to ease around him.

"*Excuse me,*" he says, moving over, and in a grand gesture

draws his arm away while he lets his hand *accidentally* slide across my breasts.

"Hey!"

"Hard nipples. I think you wanted that."

I don't answer. I just push him aside and walk back to the family room.

It takes me a while before I can calm down and concentrate on the cards. But then I finally win a hand and that brings me back to the game. Ironically I win it with a straight to the nine, seven and nine in my hand and eight, six and five on the table. And it's a big hand—even splitting it with the low, it's probably about seventy dollars. The best part about it is that Frank is one of the losers.

Now I'm beginning to get a read on the other players. Sean is the best, pretty straightforward; if he's betting he usually has it. His brother Jeff runs scared. Anyone raises, unless he has a full house he drops out. John can be tricky, but most of the time he gets pretty good cards. Sam looks like he's more interested in the potato chips than his cards. He also likes the beer and the more he drinks the sloppier his playing is. He's so sloppy it's hard to know what his cards are. And when he shares a pot with Frank, forget it, he gets really screwed. Noel is slow. Every bet takes forever like he's betting his BMW, which he managed to slip in that he just got for Christmas.

And then there's Frank. I hated him before the hallway incident, but now I loathe him. And he hates me. From right when he opened the door. I don't know what his problem is but he concentrates on me more than his cards. It's like we're playing head-to-head.

And then I get a beautiful low hand. An ace and a deuce. A possible lock if one of them doesn't turn up on board.

And so far neither one of my beauties doubles. The first card over is a ten of diamonds, then comes a jack of hearts, then a four of diamonds, and a six of spades. There's one card left to turn and everyone but Frank is out. He's been betting so strong since the flop that I read him for a low, too, but I've got the lock. I can't wait to splatter him all over the table.

Don't let the last card be an ace, please!

And it isn't. It's one of my leftover nines.

Now we're really playing head-to-head and I love it even if I do have to dip into my two hundred. He raises four dollars, I take the second raise and he takes the last one. There has to be over a hundred in the pot. A lot of it is mine but I'm getting it right back.

"I'm going low," I announce, throwing out my gorgeous ace deuce, spreading my arms and giving Frank my biggest winner's smile. Oh, do I feel good!

"No way, asshole," Frank says, putting down his straight, "there is no low. Rule of Eight, remember? The nine blew it for you. You gotta have three cards under eight out there." And he scoops up the entire pot.

My arms are still sticking out, but at least the stupid victory smile is gone. I work them down.

"Sorry. I forgot."

Everyone is nice about it. Even joking.

Not Frank. "Deal, will ya! You're ruining the game."

Now I'm beginning to lose seriously because I'm running

scared. It's Frank, he's got me so intimidated that even with promising hands I keep going out.

And he doesn't let up. Not on the cheating either. And he gets even cruder, asking me things like do I want to make a side bet, like if I lose I'll suck him off.

Every once in a while John or Sean will tell him to can it, but for the most part they're into the game and not really listening to him. Obviously, for Frank, this is not so out of character.

Sean and Jeff have to leave early so someone says, Once more around. It's okay with me because I hate the whole game and besides I'm almost out of cash. My whole Christmas money counting the fifty from my pocket is down to fifteen dollars.

I barely play the last few hands, which is probably smart since I'm back to my nines and sevens. But on the last hand I pull a pair of tens. John tells me they always play no limit on the last hand.

I'm thinking I so don't belong in this game but then a ten comes up on the flop. It has to be a sign. The up cards are a ten which gives me three tens, a seven and a four. I'm staying even if I have to play light which of course, I do.

The next card up is a king. Frank raises. Big. Could he be holding two kings?

Fifth Street is the second four. Boats are in and I have one. But if Frank really has kings, he beats me. From the way he bet, I'm not worried about the pocket fours.

There are no lows so Sean and John and Sam drop out. Jeff was out from the beginning and Noel and Frank and I are left. It's Noel's bet but he can't face the possible boats so he drops out.

It's the last hand and I'm scared. I'm in way over my head. I'm already into the pot for at least sixty dollars I don't have. I know I should get out.

I try to keep my hands leaning on the table so nobody sees how much they're shaking.

Frank gives me a real "up yours" look and pushes in all his money, which has to be at least a hundred and fifty. Sean counts it. It's a hundred and seventy. Either he's trying to bully me out or worse, he really does have the kings.

It gets very quiet because it's the biggest pot of the night and it's down to the two enemies. I really think the others want me to win because even they know Frank is such a shit.

Now it's up to me. I look at him real hard to see if there's some kind of tell. But I can't read him; he just looks vicious.

"Is this gonna take all night?" He practically spits out the question.

"Lay off her," John says, and then leans in to me. "Take your time."

I would love to beat Frank, not just because of the money— mostly because he's a cheating, mean lowlife who should be taught a lesson and it would really count coming from me. He's the kind of macho asshole who would really suffer from losing to—what did he call it? Gash.

But I'm afraid of those kings.

Somebody says something, but I don't even hear because I've got this loud buzzing in my ears. I'm holding my cards tight to the edge of the table with my elbows jammed against my body and all of me wet with sweat.

I've got my eyes fixed on Frank when I see this little flash of light to one side of his head. And then he moves and it's gone.

He leans forward and the light comes back. My eyes go there and I see it's a reflection in the shine of the toaster oven behind him.

And when he sits back up straight and raises his cards, I see them mirrored in the metal.

Two sevens.

"I'm light one seventy more." I announce and I can see everyone is stunned. Mostly Frank. "And I'm calling you," I say, resisting the ache to add "asshole," and throw down my winning tens.

"I should have watched where she got those cards," says the sore loser, trying to slip his cards into the deck without showing them.

But they won't let him.

"You mean you haven't got those kings, Frankie?" Sean says, grabbing Frank's cards and turning over his losing sevens.

And they all start to laugh. They're loving it. And me, too.

In my world I figure under the right circumstances, and these were so right they were perfect, you're allowed to cheat a cheater. Positively Cheat Street, that's what I'm thinking.

The game breaks up and Frank's out the door like a shot. The others take their time following and they're smiling and more friendly than they were all night. It's like I'm part of the group already. For sure I'm going to be asked back.

I'm the last to leave and gorgeous John walks me to the door.

"You really were hot on that last hand," he says.

"Yeah, I know." I can hardly swallow my smile.

"Too hot." He's not smiling. "Like toaster hot."

Oh God, he was sitting next to me. "You don't understand . . ." I start to explain, but he cuts me off.

"Yeah, unfortunately, I do." He pulls the door open.

I have no choice but to step out into the hall.

"See ya around," he says.

And before I can say anything else, the heavy door slams shut behind me.

Francine Pascal

Award-winning author Francine Pascal has been playing poker since . . . well, she won't say. But for many years she did battle as the only woman at a table full of men. Today, Francine divides her time between New York City and the French Riviera. She still plays poker regularly—but she is no longer the only woman at the table!

Francine's YA books—which include the bestselling Sweet Valley High and Fearless series—have sold more than 150 million copies and have been translated into twenty-five languages. Her latest novel for teens is *The Ruling Class*.

DEALING WITH THE DEVIL

by Adam Stemple

You're a card player like me, kid. I could tell just by looking at you. We don't believe in luck or gods or anything but suits and suckers and the iron-forged laws of probability. To believe anything else is a sure way to lose your roll. But I've seen some things I've got to tell, and you might be the last person I'm likely to see in this world, so I figured I better tell you.

I saw you get on the train in Dundee, same as I did. You a Scot? No? You can probably tell by my accent that I'm not either. I'm from Cincinnati originally. But my grandmother was Scottish. Loved Scotland. Never stopped yapping about it. I'd always wanted to see the place, but just never made the time. There was always a tournament running somewhere, or I was stuck and needed extra time at the tables to make my mortgage, or I just couldn't be bothered to travel overseas. But my grandmother died not too long ago, and I promised her in the hospital that I'd go to her homeland. So I guess I made this trip in her honor.

Now, Grandma was a Lamont. Had some sort of connection with Glamis Castle. I never really understood it. Some old ancestor had a charter from some other old ancestor that made him Duke of this or Earl of that. Anyway, I knew it was important to her, so I made it my first stop. Took a flight from Cincinnati to Glasgow, a train to Dundee, then took a bus from Seagate Station to the castle.

Real beautiful place, Glamis is. All those round towers with their shingled party hats on and the walls topped with those square blocks of stone.

Crenellations? That's what they're called? Thanks, kid.

Anyway, it just about took my breath away watching the castle grow bigger as the bus went up the long tree-lined drive. It wasn't like Disneyland or that fake castle casino in Vegas—it was real. And old! Older than anything I'd ever seen. Folks at the front desk said parts of it were built in the fourteenth century. There's nothing that old in the States. I stood outside just gazing up at it, feeling all the long years it had weathered washing over me. Finally, when I thought people were starting to stare, I went inside.

I loved the place. The painted and plastered ceilings, the portraits of long-dead aristocrats, the suits of armor, the tapestries. Loved everything about it. But there was one room I kept coming back to: The Crypt.

It wasn't actually a crypt; it was the servant's dining area from when the castle was first built. But with the vaulted ceiling and the walls made out of big blocks of old stone, it looked like a giant burial chamber. And there were so many dead, dusty heads and horns and antlers tacked to the walls that I felt like I was surrounded by the corpses of every hoofed animal that had ever walked the earth. To further dampen the mood, empty suits of armor stood guard near iron-barred doors, giving me the impression that if I hung around too long, I might be subjected to some barbaric form of medieval torture.

I suppose all forms of torture are barbaric, medieval or not, right, kid?

Anyway, it wasn't the look or feel of the room that kept me coming back—why would it, really? It was the story the tour guides told about it. Seems one Saturday night, a long time ago, the Earl of Glamis was running a card game. Just him and a friend, the Earl of Crawford. "Tiger," they called him, I guess.

You're smiling. Ran a few games in your time? Me, too. Great way to make some change. But they always got too big and I worried someone would try to rob them. Could've started carrying a piece, but I'm a card player not a gunfighter. Now I just play in them instead of dealing with the hassle of running them.

But the Earl, he had bigger problems than people trying to rob him. See, he wasn't allowed to play on the Sabbath. That's Sunday, in case you didn't know. And he must have been stuck a bundle to this "Tiger" Earl of Crawford, because when it got close to midnight, he was still playing. His servants begged him to stop, but he told them he'd not only play on Sunday if he pleased, he'd play with the very Devil himself. Well, midnight rolled up, and that's who showed up. The Devil.

Now, they didn't know it was the Devil at first, just a rich stranger looking to play some cards.

"Enter in the fiend's name," the Earl called out when he heard knocking at the door.

The Devil came in and sat down with a wad of cash. They dealt him in. And once they started playing, they couldn't stop. Flames rose around them, engulfing them, and still they played on.

Playing cards for all eternity. Sounds like heaven to me, not hell, but what do I know?

After a few hundred years of this, the new owners of Glamis bricked up the room. Or so the story goes. Going through the tour over and over, I heard it often enough. Sure, some of the details differed from guide to guide. Sometimes the stranger played with coins, sometimes with rubies. Sometimes the Earl was alone demanding his servants play on the Sabbath, sometimes Tiger played with him. Sometimes . . . well, it didn't matter, the basic story was always the same.

And one more thing the tour guides all agreed on: come midnight on Sundays, people said they could hear stomping and swearing and the sound of crackling flames coming from inside the walls of the Crypt.

Well, wouldn't you know it was Saturday, and I didn't have anything to do that night, so I thought I'd just go ahead and see if there was any truth to these stories about people hearing the stomping and swearing of a couple of cursed gamblers.

Why, you ask?

I'll tell you why. I've sat in every kind of poker game imaginable. From nickel-ante games with buddies when I was your age to high stakes no-limit with seasoned pros when I was older. I've played movies stars and mobsters, garbagemen and garage mechanics. I've played young and old, rich and poor in back alleys, flophouses, casinos, and cars. I've seen people play one hand and leave the table, seen others play for three days without food or sleep. I've watched people lose houses and cars and walk away smiling; I've seen guys lose their bus fare and break down in tears.

But in a million hands of poker I've never seen anyone gambling with the Devil in a room full of flames.

Not that I thought I would that night, mind you. But it seemed like a good way to pass the time.

How'd I manage to stay after the castle closed?

Well, I probably shouldn't tell a youngster like yourself, but I've always had a powerful dislike for honest work. And you can see how that might lead a fellow to learn certain sorts of skills that would keep him in cash without having to resort to punching a clock. Let's just say I used some hard-earned trade secrets to avoid cameras and curators and settled into a hiding place to wait for midnight.

I lost track of time pretty quick. Or I should say, I never really knew what the time was. I'm not a guy who regularly carries a watch. So when I heard footsteps, I thought maybe it was a guard I hadn't spotted doing his rounds. But I soon realized that the footsteps weren't approaching. They couldn't. They were coming from behind the wall to the left of the Crypt's two little windows. I emerged from my hiding place in amazement and sped to the wall.

The stories were right. Well, mostly right. I distinctly heard footsteps and voices, faint though they were through the thick wall. But the third noise wasn't crackling flames. It was riffling cards. And as I listened more, I was sure I heard coins clinking, as well.

Someone was playing cards behind those thick stone bricks.

Like I said before, I don't believe in gods or the Devil or ghosts or any of that, so I thought that I must have stumbled onto a game the guards or custodians played late at night to avoid going home to their wives, or just to pass the time.

And if there was a game going on, I wanted in.

But I couldn't just knock on the door. Or could I? I had money—a pocketful of pound notes I'd exchanged that morning—and I could play the sucker well enough. Who didn't want a rich fish at their game? And I could claim I was a friend of a friend. That gambit had worked before. No problem. With a course of action decided, I strode forward . . .

And remembered there wasn't any door.

Well, I wasn't going to let a little thing like that stop me. Not after I'd decided there was a flock of pigeons behind that wall waiting for me to come and pluck them. So I just stepped right up to the wall and pounded on it with my fist.

"Hello? Hello in there?" I called. "Angus said for me to swing by and play. You guys know Angus?"

No answer.

"He's a friend of Robert's."

Nothing.

"Come on!"

Zilch.

Plan A was foiled, but I still wanted to play. I searched along the wall for some sort of hinge or crack or hint of a door. Had as much luck as I'd had yelling. I searched in rooms around and over the Crypt, moving furniture and tapestries aside, searching for trapdoors or tunnels, anything that might lead into the card room.

Didn't find any.

Now you've probably seen all those movies where the secret passages were always reached by pulling the right book off the right shelf? Me too. I yanked the arm of every suit of armor and tweaked the nose, ears, and antlers of every dead animal in the room.

Nothing.

Then I thought of the Earl calling out for the stranger to enter in the fiend's name. And just because I was tired and frustrated and out of ideas, I stood before the wall and said loudly,

"Enter in the fiend's name!"

And the wall disappeared. Just like that. One second, a thick stone wall, the next a room full of flames with two wretched old men in ancient chairs, tattered playing cards in their hands. Behind them stood a giant red demon with black horns curled tight to his head, whipping them with a cat-o'-nine-tails as they bet and bickered and shuffled the cards to play again.

A giant red demon that was turning to see who had disturbed his work.

I ran. Out of the Crypt, out of the castle, into the courtyard. Ran up the long tree-lined drive and out to the main road. Would have run all the way to Dundee if some kind soul hadn't picked me up and driven me into town. I caught the first train out that I could, and grabbed a seat by the window in an empty car. Empty till you got on, kid. And I could tell by the way you handled that deck of cards in your hand that you were a player like me. Started thinking that maybe the Devil had spotted me before I got out of there, and that I didn't have long to live. Started thinking maybe I might want to tell someone my story.

You're nodding. Are you agreeing that may be the case or are you . . .

Say, kid, you wouldn't mind taking off your hat, would you? Thanks.

Nice horns.

I suppose we're going to play some cards now? No, you don't need to tell me what the stakes are. I think I can guess.

I'll deal.

Adam Stemple

Adam Stemple is a Minneapolis-based writer, musician, and professional poker player. He has three novels out currently, one of which, *Pay the Piper*, coauthored with Jane Yolen, just won the 2006 Locus Award for Best Young Adult Novel. He has numerous CDs out, both as a player and a producer, and plays weekends with his Irish rebel band, The Tim Malloys. And as a poker player, he recently won the $300 No Limit Holdem event at the 2005 Canterbury Park Fall Poker Classic, and can often be found playing online at a number of sites under the moniker hatfield13. Stop by and say hello.

THE CARDS THAT ARE HIDDEN

by Alex Flinn

It was bad news again.

"How was your night?" Britt's mom said, turning off Letterman, when Rick finally came in.

"She means how much did you lose?" Britt added, helpfully.

Rick looked at Mom. "Does she need to be here?"

"I was here before you." Britt noticed that Rick's blue eyes were bloodshot. He'd been drinking.

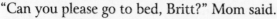

"Can you please go to bed, Britt?" Mom said.

Britt went, but she could still hear them arguing through the apartment's paper-thin walls. Mom had promised they'd buy a house as soon as she and Rick got married. But they weren't married yet, and Britt for one was glad. She'd figured Rick was just a boy toy, and he'd be gone soon enough. And yet, Mom wouldn't throw him out, even on nights like tonight when he lost most of their money gambling.

Her mother's voice. "We have to talk—"

"I don't want to talk about it!"

"The electric's due, and the phone. I have to know how much you lost."

A pause. "Not that much."

"But you did lose? Again?"

No shit, Sherlock. He always loses. That's because he's a loser. Sometimes, Britt wished he'd just be violent. If Rick would hit her mother, she'd be sure to throw him out. It would be easier than this slow bleeding death.

"I'll win it back next time," Rick said.

"Next time? Do you really think—?"

"I said leave me alone!"

Silence for a minute. But only a minute. Then, Rick's voice. "Thing is . . ."

"The thing?" her mother demanded. "There's a thing?"

"Thing is, I owe a little."

"How little?"

Rick said the amount so softly Britt couldn't hear it. She did hear her mom gasp.

"Oh, Rick," she said. "We don't have it."

"I have to pay him, Kath."

"Or what? They won't let you play anymore? That would be a good thing."

"It's a matter of honor."

In her room, Britt laughed out loud. Rick had honor, huh?

"I can't welsh on a bet," he said. "I'd never live it down."

But taking your girlfriend's money that was meant to feed her and her kid, that's honorable?

Mom didn't say that, though, and after a few more back and forths, Britt heard the sound of Mom's purse scraping against the kitchen counter. *Stupid!*

Rick had won even though he'd lost.

Friday was a pep rally day. Britt loved Fridays because she could wear her cheerleader uniform. In her blue-and-white Palmetto Panthers uniform, Britt could pretend she was still just a cute girl, a cool girl with no problems. Britt knew as well as Rick that sometimes the cards that weren't showing made all the difference. But most of her friends didn't, so if Britt dressed cute and acted like nothing was wrong, they believed her. It's not like they had any problems.

Before Rick, Britt and her mother had done okay. Sure, Mom was single, and her dad was MIA, child support–wise. And yes, they lived in an apartment while most of her friends had McMansions with pools, on the other side of the highway. But Mom made good money as a nurse, enough at least to buy Britt decent clothes. So Britt didn't have to show the bad cards she'd been dealt.

But that was before Rick.

Since Rick, there'd been no money for clothes or lunches at

McDonald's, or pretty much anything extra. For a while, Britt had paid for them herself by babysitting. That was, until she realized she needed to save for cheerleading camp next summer. So now, her clothes were mostly old or from Tar-jay. She hoped her friends hadn't noticed, but she knew they did.

But Fridays, pep rally days, were okay.

When Britt got to first period, she perched on her desk so everyone could see the grandeur of her uniform. Britt Davis, cheergirl, not a care in the world. As people came in, Britt went into overdrive, tossing her blonde, Supercuts hairstyle and laughing, just to let everyone see what a good time she was having.

That was, until *he* came in.

He was Josh Myers. Josh was a *player,* not just a *playa,* Palmetto High's answer to a professional gambler. Britt had seen him playing cards outside at lunchtime—for "funsies" as far as the adults were concerned, but everyone else knew money was changing hands . . . mostly going into Josh's hands.

Britt didn't like Josh. His gambling made him a charter member of Future Scumbags of America.

But more important, Josh looked at Britt. A lot. And he talked to her too. Normally, a guy like Josh Myers wouldn't dare talk to someone like Britt. It made Britt wonder if Josh could really see her, could see through the good cards that were showing to the lousy ones that were hidden.

"Hey, Britt," Josh called when he got to her desk.

"Hey." Britt looked for someone else to talk to. But her friends weren't there yet. Mom had dropped her off early, before her shift. Most of her friends didn't roll in until 7:29. Britt could get a ride, but that would mean letting them see where she lived.

Josh leaned his hand against Britt's desk. "How's it going?"

"Good." *Go away.*

"Ready for the *Great Gatsby* test?"

"Sure." She stuck with monosyllables, hoping he'd get a clue. Britt could blow Josh off, but she couldn't be rude. He was cute, tall, with dark hair and blue eyes. Her friends considered him a harmless loser, not a major sleaze. Lots of guys she knew took part in his card games. Only Britt could see the dark underbelly.

"You look so hot in that uniform." Josh leaned closer.

"Thanks." Britt glanced at the clock. Five more minutes.

"I look forward to seeing you in it every Friday."

"Yep." So he'd been watching her. *No, stupid.* Friday was pep rally day. Everyone knew that.

"You know, I was wondering . . ."

Britt's eyes flew to the door. He was going to ask her out. *Bail! Bail!*

". . . Saturday night?" Josh was finishing.

"No," Britt said, even though she hadn't heard most of what he'd said.

"But—"

"Babysitting. Sorry." Six whole syllables. She felt she owed him that. After all, he wasn't actually gambling away his girlfriend's rent payment. Not yet.

"Babysitting?" He looked incredulous.

"Every Saturday. Hey, some of us actually need to earn money." It was an admission she'd never have made to one of her friends. But she didn't much care what Josh thought.

"Tell me about it," he said. "It's hard, keeping up with the rich kids in this place. That's why I started my little business. I bet you and I have lots in common . . ." He moved closer, completely violating Britt's personal space.

"Teacher's here!" Britt announced. "Better get to your seat."

She said this loud enough that people looked over at them, and Josh backed off.

Britt really did have to babysit Saturday. Cheerleading camp was six hundred dollars, and it was mandatory if you were on the squad. Last summer, Mom had paid, but she'd put in the deposit before Rick moved in. This year, Britt worried that they wouldn't have money for it, and she wasn't getting kicked out of cheer. That would be the ultimate humiliation. So she had a regular job every Saturday, and sometimes Mrs. Poznaski hired her after school too. She'd already saved more than half of what she needed, and it was only November.

When she came in from her job Saturday, she tucked two twenties into her secure hiding place, a purse in the back of her closet. In the living room, Mom and Rick were at it again.

"Please, Kathy, you said yourself you don't like it that much."

Like what that much? Britt went into the bathroom to brush her teeth.

"That's not the point, Rick," her mother said. "I don't feel right, selling Mom's ring."

"It's just a pawn. I'll get it back in a week."

"That's what you said about my bracelet, and I never got it back."

Britt ran the water onto her toothbrush, but she couldn't drown out Rick's voice. "My name will be mud if I don't pay."

♣

There was a pause before her mother said, "I don't care."

They kept arguing back and forth, and Britt got into bed with the pillow over her head. Finally, the arguing stopped, and Britt knew it was because Mom had given in.

The next morning, Sunday, while Britt was eating breakfast, Rick came in and sat with her. Mom had already gone to work.

"Late night babysitting, huh?"

"Yep." Britt was giving Rick the Josh treatment.

"Make a lot of money?"

Britt spooned puffed rice into her mouth and grunted. She knew where this was going.

Rick tried again. "So what's the going rate for sitters these days?"

"Why? You plan on getting a babysitting job?"

Rick laughed and finished his toast before speaking again. "Hey, I just thought of something. I should teach you to play poker."

"What?"

"Yeah, I read that kids your age are really into Texas Holdem. It'd be fun, sort of a bonding experience."

Except I hate you, and you're trying to take my money.

"I don't think so."

"You sure?"

"Sure."

Rick thought a minute. "Well if you change your mind . . ."

"I won't."

After Rick left, she called Mom at the hospital.

"Britt, you know I can't talk at work."

Britt knew that. She also knew that calling at work was the

only way to get a word in. After all, Mom couldn't yell or cry or storm away from the phone at the nurse's station, like she did when Britt tried to talk to her at home.

"Your boyfriend just tried to get money from me," she said.

A pause. "Well, maybe—"

"Maybe what? Maybe there was a really good game going on? I'm saving my money, saving for clothes, cheer camp, college— things you can't afford because of Rick."

"Britt, I can't discuss this right now."

"Are you so desperate for a man that you can't see he's using you?"

Another pause. Finally, Britt's mom said, "We can talk when I get home," and hung up.

But Britt knew they'd never talk.

Later that day, Britt walked into her room and stopped. She'd been out all day. Now, the bed, which she'd made before leaving, was rumpled. Stuff was out of the closet, and the drawers were partly opened. She ran to the closet. The all-important purse, which she'd left snapped tight, was unsnapped.

Honorable, huh?

Britt patted her pocket. Lucky she'd taken the money with her.

But she didn't come out of her room until the next morning, for school. She took her money with her then too. Sure, there were thieves at school, especially in the locker room, so she'd have to cram $417 in her shoe during cheer practice. But it was safer than at home.

In English, Josh asked her out again, for Friday after the game this time.

"Aren't gamblers supposed to be good at reading people's faces?" she said. "You'd think you could take a hint."

But Tuesday at lunch, when she saw Josh playing his game, she started thinking. Maybe he could help her.

Britt walked over to his spot, under the stairs. He was playing with a bunch of guys who looked like freshmen, and he had a stack of pennies in front of him, so it looked like they were just playing for pennies. But Britt guessed the pennies were chips, and they were playing for more.

"I need to talk to you," she said.

Josh dealt another card to each player. "And why would you want to talk to me? Correction—why would I want to talk to you after yesterday?"

Britt started to answer, but Josh held up his hand for silence. They were betting again. When they finished, Britt said, "I have a proposition for you." *That should get his attention.*

"Okay, I'm interested." He turned to the freshmen. "Next hand's the last one."

Josh won the hand, judging from the groaning, but folded early in the next. Then, there was some business of everyone trading their pennies for dollars with Josh getting most of them. "Same time tomorrow," he called as he walked toward a bench on the side of the school.

"How much did you make?" Britt asked.

"About thirty dollars. Not bad for fifteen minutes' work."

Not bad at all. Britt would have to babysit a whole evening to make that much. But, she reminded herself, babysitting was honest work.

"What'd you want to talk about?" Josh asked.

"I want you to teach me to play poker."

Josh laughed. "Thinking of starting your own business?"

Britt wrinkled her nose. "Nah." She explained about Rick, her mom's money, him asking to teach her poker, and her plan.

Josh nodded. "And you think that would work?"

"He keeps saying he'd never welsh. He'll be expecting me to be an easy mark. That's why I need you to teach me."

"What's in it for me?" There was a smile in Josh's blue eyes.

Britt had hoped just spending time with her would be enough to please Josh. But she'd decided that if it wasn't, she'd make the sacrifice.

"If I win, I'll go out with you."

"How many times?"

"One?"

Josh kept smiling.

"Okay, twice," she said. "But we're just going out. I'm not agreeing to . . . anything else."

"In that case, three times, and we have a deal."

"Done." She didn't want to go out with Josh, who was, after all, a career gambler. But she wasn't like her mother. She could resist a gambler's eyes, even if they were the bluest ones she'd ever seen.

"Texas Holdem's a game of strategy," Josh said, shuffling together two decks of cards. Britt watched his hands. The fingers were long and skinny and the cards seemed to fly between them on their own.

He saw her looking at him. "Think I could be a dealer in Vegas?"

Britt shrugged. "Depends. Are they hiring geeky seventeen-year-olds?"

They'd met at his apartment, in the same crappy neighborhood as Britt's own. This surprised Britt. She realized that Josh, like herself, wasn't showing all the cards he had.

The basic rules of Texas Holdem were easy, Josh explained. Each player got two cards facedown. "Hole cards," Josh called them. Then, there were five community cards shared by all players. "You make your hand out of the best five cards out of the seven."

"But how do you win if everyone shares the same cards?"

"That's where strategy comes in. You have to look at the cards, not just in terms of what they can do for you, but also what they mean for your opponent." When Britt gave him a blank look, he said, "You'll see."

He dealt Britt her two hole cards, a queen of diamonds and a king of spades. Britt knew these were good cards. Everyone knew face cards were good. But she didn't smile. She knew that much too.

"So this is where you decide whether to start betting," Josh said. "If you don't have a pair, or at least two cards ten or above at this point, you should probably get out. But we'll do a few practice hands before we worry about betting."

He dealt three more cards, faceup, a king of hearts, ten of spades, and a six of spades. "This is the flop. You bet again now, or get out."

Britt checked the chart Josh had printed from the Internet. It showed the ranking of poker hands. She already had a pair, and there were still two more cards. Britt tried not to smile. Maybe she was just lucky at cards.

Josh was talking. "If you don't have at least a high pair by this point, you need to cut your losses."

Britt nodded, trying to look grave.

The next card was a nine of hearts, then a queen of hearts. *Yesss!* Britt knew it was okay to smile when she flipped up her cards. "Two pair. Read 'em and weep."

Josh laughed. "I'll read 'em, but I won't weep." He turned up his cards, and Britt gaped. A ten and jack of hearts. He put them with the king, queen, and nine of hearts from the community cards. "Straight flush to the king."

Britt laughed, glad they hadn't been playing for money. It was like Josh had said—she hadn't thought about what his cards might be.

"There's nothing you could've done about that," Josh said. "Two pair, especially both face cards, is a good hand. I just had a better one. Usually, the winning hand will be better than a pair, but sometimes, you luck out and win with less. Other times, you have a good hand, but your opponent's is better.

"Oh," he said, "and you need to work on your poker face. I could tell the whole time that you had a good hand. I try and think about something sad."

"I'll think about death," Britt said, laughing.

"Think about your mom staying with this scumbag."

They played a bunch more hands, and Josh talked about when to bet and when to fold. "Don't stay in the hand just because you're in it. That's what suckers do. But don't be a chicken either."

After what seemed like a hundred hands, Josh sent Britt home with two decks of cards and instructions to practice constantly. "Just deal cards to yourself and your imaginary friend and try to decide whether to bet. Poker's a lot about luck. The strategy part's knowing if you're winning."

"I'll practice all night long," Britt said.

"That's good." Josh smiled. "I want you to win."

They got together Wednesday and Thursday after cheer practice, and Friday, after school, before the game. In between, Britt dealt herself hundreds of imaginary hands, then tried to predict whether they were winners.

Friday, Josh said, "I have an SAT prep class tomorrow. Are you going too?"

Britt shrugged. "Can't afford it." Just another way Rick had screwed up her life.

"Guess how I got the dollars to pay for the class," Josh said.

"Cheating freshmen at lunchtime?"

"Hey, I don't cheat to win. And the kids I play with are rich. I'm not. I gamble to pay for college."

"You're not worried you'll get addicted to it?" Britt asked, thinking of Rick.

"If I get good enough SAT scores for a scholarship, I'm done. If not, I'll have to gamble through college. But no, I'm not planning on making it a profession. I've got a four-point-five GPA."

Britt hoped she had a good enough poker face not to show that her own GPA was significantly lower. Josh must have been taking more than just honors English. He hadn't impressed her as a big brain, but maybe it took brains to win at poker. That would go a long way toward explaining why Rick always lost.

"So when's the big game?" he asked.

"Tuesday. My mom's going out of town for a conference and

leaving me with Rick. I told him that would be the perfect time for him to teach me poker."

"Remember, you have to let him win the first few hands," Josh said. "Or, at least, make some stupid mistakes—like betting on a bad hand. That'll get him to loosen up with the money later on."

"I get it."

"And here." Josh reached into his pocket and pulled out something. He held it out, and Britt realized it was a stack of ones, maybe fifty of them.

"I can't."

"Take it. In case of emergency."

"But it's your money."

"It's a loan, okay? I want to help you. I want you to win."

Britt smiled. "Why do you want to go out with me so much?"

Josh shrugged. "I like you. You're not like the other girls. You have . . . opinions on things."

"Even if my opinion is I don't like guys who gamble?"

He shrugged again. "You've got your reasons. And if you go out with me, I'll get a chance to change your mind." He held the bills out again. "Just for an emergency. You'll be sorry if you need it and don't take it."

Britt pocketed the bills. "I'll pay you back."

Josh smiled. "I hope so. Because that'll mean you won."

It was too easy. Tuesday night, as soon as the door closed behind Mom, Rick was knocking on Britt's door. "You still want me to teach you poker?"

Behind the door, Britt hesitated, like she hadn't been planning to ask him the exact same thing. "Um, sure. Let me just . . . I'll be there in a second."

She went to the closet and took out the purse, which held every cent she had, close to five hundred dollars, including her babysitting money and Josh's fifty. She'd broken it into small bills, mostly ones and fives. She wouldn't let Rick know how much she had. She went to the dining room and sat down at the table. "Okay."

Rick smiled and shuffled the decks of cards. The dining room table was white mica; since Rick had moved in, it had gotten pitted and cracked, because he put his feet up when Mom wasn't home. Rick held the deck out for Britt to cut.

"So how do you play?" she asked.

"The best thing is to learn as you go," Rick said. He dealt each of them two cards. "These are your hole cards," he said. "First round of betting comes now."

"I bet even though I don't know how to play? How do I know if they're good cards?"

Rick smiled like Britt was a second grader who'd asked about the Tooth Fairy. "Oh, at this point, you pretty much bet. You can't really tell until after the flop."

Britt put in a dollar before even looking at her cards. Then she looked at them. A three of clubs and an eight of spades. Terrible hand. Rick put in a dollar of his own, then dealt three cards faceup, two jacks and a seven. Now, Britt had a pair. But so did Rick. Still, she bet another dollar. "This is fun," she said.

The next two cards were an eight of hearts and a king of diamonds. That gave Britt two pair, but when it came time to show her cards, Britt told Rick, "I just have that one pair."

"Aw, that's all right," Rick said, showing a pair of sevens and sweeping in the pot—including Britt's four dollars. "You're just starting. Bet you'll do better next time."

But of course, Rick didn't give her any tips like Josh had. And Britt let him win the first five hands—including one where she folded with a full house—until Rick had twenty dollars of her money.

"Wow, I'm not very lucky today," she said. But she knew it was time to start playing for real.

On the sixth hand, Rick dealt Britt a pair of queens.

"So, do you usually bet so low?" Britt said.

"Nah, I was trying to go easy on you."

Britt shrugged. "Maybe I'd be luckier if I bet more." She put a five into the pot.

Rick glanced at his own hand, and put in a five. He dealt a ten, a five, and a queen. Now, Britt had three queens. She put in another five.

"Are you sure you know what you're doing?" Rick said, calling her five.

Britt laughed. "No. But even if you win, it's all in the family, right? I'm just paying your gambling debts."

Rick laughed. "Guess so." He dealt another queen, and Britt put in another five. When the last up-card was an ace, Rick could barely conceal his smile as Britt put in a final five.

"Sorry, kiddo," he said, showing his cards—he had a pair of aces and the pair of queens. "Two pair."

"Aww, that stinks," Britt said, showing her queens. "Does four of a kind beat two pair, or the other way around?"

Rick stared at Britt's cards, muttered a curse word, then shoved the pot at Britt. "Lucky hand."

"Sure." But Britt smiled. She'd won back her twenty.

From then on, Britt played for real. She mostly won or, if she had a bad hand, she folded early so she didn't lose that much. In short time, she'd won ninety dollars in addition to Rick's twenty.

"Wow, this is fun," she said.

Rick grimaced. "Yeah, fun."

"How much money did you have?" she asked him, shuffling the deck on the pitted mica.

"Hundred to start." Rick pulled the bills from his pocket. "Ten now."

"Oh, wow," Britt said. "Maybe we should stop. I wouldn't want to take all your money."

Josh had told her to say this. No way would Rick want Britt, a sixteen-year-old girl, pitying him. He wouldn't fold. He'd just try harder.

"Nah, you're just lucky," he said, like Josh had said he would. "It can't last."

Britt let him win the next hand, one she'd have folded on ordinarily. But she won the one after that, and the next hand, Rick bet with an IOU.

"Shouldn't we stop?" Britt said. "You already owe me ten. How do I know you're good for it?" She stood and started to walk away.

"I'm good for it." Rick grabbed Britt's wrist and pulled. "I never welsh."

"Hey," Britt said, pulling her hand away. "Let go of me."

"You can't just take my money. Don't be a bitch."

Britt laughed, seeing him getting desperate. "I won it."

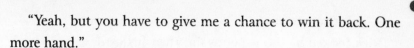

"Yeah, but you have to give me a chance to win it back. One more hand."

Britt sat back down.

She won another hundred. Then two hundred—all in IOUs. She stood again. "I want to quit now."

Rick started after her, grabbing for her arm again. "Please. Just one more hand."

"Go away!"

"Just one more hand!" He was yelling now.

Britt stared at him. She had him where she wanted him. But would he take her bait? She looked into his desperate gambler's eyes and guessed he would.

"Okay, one more hand. But not for an IOU. For something else."

His smile dropped. "What, then?"

"Deal."

Rick smiled and dealt the two hole cards. Britt could see he'd do anything. "Something more interesting. I'll bet the two hundred you owe me. We're even if you win. But if I win, you have to do what I want." She took out the paper where they'd been keeping track of Rick's IOUs. She put it on the table, covering up a big pit in the mica.

Rick stared at it. He smiled. "And what's that?"

Britt looked right into Rick's eyes. They couldn't stay off the IOU more than a second.

"If I win this hand," she said, "you'll move out. You'll write a letter to my mom, telling her you got together with an old girlfriend, and you'll be gone when she gets home Thursday."

Rick laughed. "Right."

"I'm totally serious."

Rick looked at the paper again, then his cards. He nodded. "Put in the other hundred."

As soon as he said it, Britt realized her mistake. She'd spoken too soon. He must have a good hand, and then her scheme was ruined. But it was too late. She nodded and dealt. Rick glanced at the cards and smiled. He didn't need a poker face, after all, since she'd already bet. "You are so beat," he said.

Britt groaned and dealt the flop—jack of clubs, jack of hearts, ten of hearts. Now, she had a pair. But so did Rick.

She dealt the fourth community card, a queen of spades. Rick grinned harder. She knew he had good cards, maybe another pair or three of a kind, the way he was grinning.

But when she dealt the fifth community card, Britt looked at Rick. She wanted to slap that shit-eating grin off his face.

"You first," she said.

Rick laughed and turned his cards over. "My pair of queens makes a full house—queens and jacks."

"Ugh," Britt groaned.

"Hard to beat," Rick said. "But maybe you can win it back on another hand. You didn't really want me to leave, did you?"

Britt shrugged. Then she turned over her own cards, the king and ace of hearts.

She put the three together with ten of hearts, jack of hearts, and the last community card.

The queen of hearts.

Ten of hearts, jack of hearts, queen of hearts, king of hearts, ace of hearts.

"I forget," she said. "Does a royal flush beat a full house?"

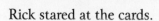

Rick stared at the cards.

"You . . . you bitch. You cheated . . . somehow."

"I got lucky."

"Yeah." Rick laughed, a sick, thudding laugh. "You got lucky. Just luck. Let's play another hand—double or nothing."

Britt shook her head. "You're out of money. Way out." She yawned. "And I'm tired. Besides, you have to know when to quit."

"But . . . you can't . . . I can't . . ."

Britt withdrew a sheet of typing paper from her purse. "I have the letter here for you to sign."

"What?"

"The one for my mom."

"You . . ." Rick was practically hyperventilating. "You planned this? You can't do this. You can't make me move out."

"I can't make you. But you will. You always said you never welsh on a bet. What would my mom say if she knew you welshed on this one, after she used our rent money to pay off your other bets?"

Rick grabbed for her purse. "You . . . one more hand! One more hand!"

"Sign the letter," Britt said, "and I'll give you back your hundred dollars. For a hotel. I'll even give you fifty of my money." She was feeling generous. After all, she wasn't going to have to save so much anymore, now that Rick would be gone.

"You little bitch," he whispered.

But finally, he signed the letter and went into the bedroom to pack his stuff in two big boxes Britt had thoughtfully gotten him. After he left, Britt would put the letter on her mother's pillow.

And tomorrow, she'd take her savings and change the locks on the apartment doors. Rick had given her his keys, but Britt didn't trust him.

But now, even though it was nearly midnight, Britt dialed Josh's number.

"Were you sleeping?" she said when he answered.

"I was waiting to hear from you." She could hear his smile when he realized it was her. "How'd we do?"

"We won," she said. "You won the bet."

He laughed. "Does that mean you'll go out with me?"

Britt heard Rick, walking toward the door. "I guess. Fair's fair."

"Right. Fair's fair." Josh was silent a moment. Then, he cleared his throat. "Look, you don't have to go out with me if you don't want. I'm not going to force you. Just give me back my fifty bucks, and we'll call it even. Okay?"

Britt heard Rick open and close the front door. She walked into the living room with the portable phone.

"That's okay," she said. "I want to go out with you."

She smiled, realizing it was true.

Then she turned the dead bolt on the front door.

Alex Flinn

Alex Flinn learned to play video poker on a college trip to Las Vegas with her parents, and has honed her gambling skills at charity casino nights all over her hometown of Miami, Florida. However, her preferred game is Blackjack. She is the author of several young-adult novels, including *Breathing Underwater, Fade to Black,* and *Diva.* Her newest book, *Beastly,* is a modern, urban Beauty and the Beast story. Visit her on the Web at www.alexflinn.com.

SPORTIN' MEN

by Gary Phillips

"Be careful, Junie, you ain't old enough to handle that yet."

"Don't sell the boy short, Brim, remember how you were at his age." Mercer Cooke and the other men at the table laughed. The teenage Glen Murray, called Junie, had been caught gawking by his uncle at one of Miss Zenobia's party girls.

Cooke held out a couple of dollar bills

to the teenager. "Mix me a Jack and Coke, would you, youngster? And fetch me a hamhock sandwich, son. Slap some hogshead cheese on it too." He saw and upped the raise by ten dollars.

"Okay, Mr. Cooke," Junie said, his cheeks still warm. The liquor and such was on a sideboard and he took care of the drink order. Then he went off toward the kitchen in the restored antebellum colonial mansion. This meant leaving the parlor where the game was going, dealer's choice. This also meant having to pass by the girl he'd tried to peek at on the sly when she walked past. Well, she must be at least four years older than him, he figured, which made her twenty and, he supposed, a woman. For she was certainly more experienced than he was.

"How come they calls you Junie?" the girl he'd been transfixed by asked when he entered the area off the parlor that Miss Zenobia called the foyer. A fancy ballroom chandelier hung from its ceiling. And this space was bigger than what Junie had for sleeping at his uncle's place.

She and the other one, whose name was Tanya, were sitting on a couch in the room containing the two pool tables and the plasma TV. They were playing the AlienQuake II video game on the set. Tanya blew a megadroid's head off, earning her bonus points. Both of them were dressed in silky undergarments and short untied satiny robes. They looked like honeys fresh from a BET rap video. How could he not peep that when she'd walked into the parlor to whisper something to Valentine Lewis, one of the players?

" 'Cause you was called Junebug when you were small?" the girl-woman asked, invading the young man's reverie.

"My mother and older brother were both born in June," the smitten teen answered.

"And so were you?"

He got lost in her eyes. "No. September."

She frowned and chewed a little on her lower lip, and a rainbow of lights popped inside his head.

"This is Missa, she just stared this week," Tanya said, her thumbs furiously working the control's toggles.

"Glad to meet you," he managed without stammering. "I've got to get something," he added and scooted away. He could hear them whispering as he went, and they laughed that laugh that fine females do when they know they're messing with a dude's mind. At least his cheeks weren't warm again.

In the kitchen he deftly separated the meat from the shank to make Mr. Cooke's sandwich. Miss Zenobia entered as he started out. She'd just come back from some business she had to attend to and was wearing one of her crowns, one of her flamboyant hats, the kind that black women of a certain age wore to church. This one was a volcanic eruption of peacock feathers and rhinestones. Junie was sure Miss Zenobia hadn't been to church in many years. But he'd seen a deacon or two in the poker game, who headed upstairs afterward with one of the heavenly wonders, as Uncle Brim would crack.

Behind Miss Zenobia was her driver and number one of two bodyguards, the crosstown bus–sized Peteypeet. He was trying to be cool while eyeing the prize Junie was carrying on a saucer.

"How are things, young man?" Miss Zenobia asked.

"Fine, ma'am, just fine." He wanted to get out of there, but there was no way to simply ease past them. The madam was of some size around, and Peteypeet was like an anchored battleship at the open swing door.

"Aren't you already a junior?"

"Yes, that's right. I turn seventeen in about a month."

She smiled and removed some folded bills from her protruding bosom. "Put that toward your college fund." She handed him the money. "Brim is all right for who he is, but you've got imagination, Junie. You can go somewhere and not wind up here."

"Thank you," Junie said, getting by the two of them. He looked at the money; it was two one-hundred-dollar bills. Oh, man. Now he was not only nervous, but feeling even worse about what he and Uncle Brim were about to do. He was sure glad he hadn't checked the wireless remote he'd previously plugged in behind the refrigerator.

"I guess I'll have to throw my gat on them," Uncle Brim had said when he told Junie what he intended to do.

"There's a better way," the young man advised. They went to the public library and, online, he showed his devious uncle a site about high-tech homes. At Circuit City, they bought a radio frequency device that controlled lights.

"If it goes black at the right moment, then getting away shouldn't be that hard while everybody runs into each other."

"Good to see you get something out of school, nephew," he'd said, shaking his head appreciatively. "Damn sure more than just filling a seat like I did."

And tonight was the night. Uncle Brim owed some serious money to some impatient types. Junie didn't know what-all for, but what else could he do? His mother, a crack addict, had sunk into the netherworld. His father had died years before in a prison fight, and Brimfeld Lee, his mother's brother, was the only family to take him in. He was going to do the robbery regardless,

Brim had told Junie, so he had to help and hope that nobody got hurt. Junie knew if he did nothing, Miss ·Zenobia wouldn't believe he wasn't in on it. And he couldn't snitch on his uncle, so he was stuck.

The two hundred weighed like iron in his pocket. He placed the snack at Mr. Cooke's elbow. Miss Zenobia had been good and fair with him. His uncle had gotten him this job of keeping the players supplied with their refreshments, and running the occasional errand to the store. He worked Thursdays and Fridays after school and on weekends. If it came to rough stuff involving a drunk or a "belligerent second floor patron," as Miss Zenobia would say, Peteypeet or Hiram, the other bodyguard, took care of that.

And now he was going to not only spit on her kindness, but do this crime that would change his life forever. His uncle had to leave town. Junie wasn't stupid. He knew Brim wasn't about to pay these others he owed—others Brim was even more scared of than Miss Zenobia. What would Junie do about school? And where would they live? His uncle only mumbled incomplete sentences to these questions. The robbery was the only thing commanding his attention.

The game wound down and it got to be time for the last hand.

"Omaha, high-low, eight or better for low," stated the dealer, Valentine Lewis, who owned a used car lot.

"I can only play two from my hand?" Morris King asked. With his sister he ran the family's funeral parlor, and was considered an expert embalmer. Uncle Brim picked up stiffs for him now and then for extra money.

"Right, the cards speak," Elliot Harris said. He was a small-boned, light-skinned black man who managed a popular seafood restaurant and had taught mathematics at the university level. It was rumored that he was a silent partner with Miss Zenobia in her establishment.

The four down cards were dealt to each, Junie watching the faces and bodies of the players for their tells, the unconscious giveaways that indicated good, bad or so-so cards. As usual, his uncle, Mr. Cooke and Mr. Lewis' faces were like ancient masks on display in a museum. Sometimes just to get in the heads of the others, his uncle would smile broadly when he had no chance of making anything. The embalmer sniffed and that meant he had something decent, a pair or an ace. And Mr. Harris might as well show his cards, given his sour look. He folded on the first round of betting.

On the flop, turning over the first three cards, Mr. Lewis gripped the back of his neck and cracked it. The action wasn't a tell. He did that routinely, the stiffness a by-product of getting T-boned a few years ago in his Caddy by a cheerleader in a Trans Am paying more attention to talking on her cell phone than driving.

His uncle raised, and raised again when the bet came back around to him. The others knew that didn't indicate he was holding anything of value, as Brim liked to bluff, often recklessly. "You better know they hang low on me, baby," he was found of bragging to Junie and anyone else he could regale. "I ain't scared of no motherlover in this world or the next."

The turn, the fourth card over, was a ten of clubs. There was a nine of clubs, a jack of hearts and a three of diamonds already exposed.

"No low possible," Mercer Cooke announced.

Betting resumed. Junie's uncle bet strong, putting twelve dollars in the pot. What did it matter to him? He was going to take it all anyway. The fifth card, Fifth Street, the river, was a jack of clubs. Mr. Cooke bet the maximum. Uncle Brim and Valentine called. The undertaker threw his cards in.

"Pot's right," Mr. Cooke declared. There was three hundred and forty on the table. The players showed. Valentine Lewis had a king-high flush with the clubs.

"That beats me," Mercer Cooke said, showing his two jacks to give him three-of-a-kind.

"But not me," Uncle Brim said, beaming. He showed the ace and deuce of clubs, giving him the highest flush. "That's a good sign," he breathed as he raked in the chips, winking at Junie standing nearby.

"Well." Mr. King sighed, looking toward the doorway where Missa waited. "I'm tapped out." She retreated, snickering. "For cards that is."

As was the procedure, the bank, which was Miss Zenobia, cashed out the players, after taking her customary cut. She'd been away when the game started, and Hiram had initially gathered the buy-in monies. He reappeared. Hiram was tall and long-limbed to Peteypeet's stocky width. He'd been a jailer in the past, and was known to favor knives as his choice of inflicting discipline.

Everybody stood and stretched. Junie moved toward the archway. Miss Zenobia was probably upstairs but he didn't know where the hulking Peteypeet might be. If he was in the kitchen fixing himself food, that would cut off their escape route and access to the stash. Once, when the water heater had busted, Junie had spied Miss Zenobia lifting a loose board out of the kitchen floor to take out a healthy stack of bills. This was underneath the standing cutting board. That was the real goal of Uncle Brim. Why had Junie been such a big mouth and told him about that?

"Sweet dreams, gents, till next week," Uncle Brim said after getting his money and good-byes were said all around. "I've got to squeeze the lizard." He headed for the bathroom that was situated at the end of the foyer, and thus closer to the kitchen and his goal.

Junie began cleaning up the parlor and counting in his head. Hiram drifted away. Mr. Cooke and Mr. Lewis were hanging around, chatting with Tanya and Missa. They were married men and never journeyed upstairs. "They're window-shopping," Uncle Brim would say. "Old whiskers like the attention of young things but their hearts couldn't take the strain if they really tried to do anything." He'd laugh roughly.

Junie counted to a slow forty and pushed the button on the electronic tab in his pocket. The lights went out, a bulb popped, and the shouting began.

"Pay your electric bill, Zenobia," Mercer Cooke joked.

Junie called out, "I'll check the circuit breaker."

"I'll go with you," the gruff voice of Peteypeet said.

"Sure," he said to throw off suspicion. "Where are you?"

"Over here," the bodyguard said, flicking on his lighter.

Junie came over to him. As they headed toward the kitchen, there was a crash of a body and cursing. Junie had carried one of the chairs with him, placing it in the way of where he remembered the men had been talking with the females. At various times during the last two weeks, he'd practiced going from the parlor to the back of the house with his eyes closed to memorize the layout.

"You better see about that," Junie suggested to the large man.

Peteypeet's pissed look was illuminated by the tiny flame of his plastic liquor store lighter. But he knew if he didn't go back and one of the customers was hurt, he'd get chewed out by Miss Zenobia. "Stay put," he ordered and turned around. The little light bounced from side to side with the bruiser's gait, and disappeared into the archway. Junie was already at the back door off the rear stairs once used by the maid.

"What's up?" a voice called and he almost fainted. Missa came close, and he could hear her satiny robe fluttering open.

"I've got to go."

She put a hand on his arm. A current shot through him. She intoxicated him. "What are you two up to? I know Brim just lit out of here. I couldn't tell directly, but by the light of the moon it looked to me like he was carrying something."

"I don't—"

Missa put a finger to his lips. "I get a share or I yell."

"If I'm caught, you won't get anything," Junie whispered urgently. He could hear Peteypeet rumbling closer.

Her head down, Missa smiled crookedly up at him and said, "How can I trust you?" And then she kissed him. Kissed him like he'd seen in the movies, and so much better than the couple of girls he'd kissed in school.

"The Eden Motel," he breathed and jumped over the back steps. He dived into the open back window of his uncle's old-school '74 Pontiac Catalina with the panties hanging from the rearview mirror. Uncle Brim righted the boat of a car, and they tore off toward the highway in the humid night.

Looking back, Junie saw Peteypeet bang the rear screen door so hard it busted loose from the top hinge. He just stood there staring, a sweet little ugly smile of determination on his sweating face.

After two hours of the road, the two thieves arrived at the Castle Rock Motel off Route 40 across the county line. Junie had been thunderstruck, but not so naïve he would tell Missa where they were really headed.

"Not as much as I hoped," Uncle Brim complained, after re-counting the nine thousand seven hundred dollars, a thousand two hundred of which came from the poker game. "Zenobia must have had to make some payoffs lately. I know the new District Attorney has been making noise about cracking down." He paced, hands on his hips. "I can't get far enough on this fast enough." He looked around and then pawed through the equipment bag he'd previously packed with clothes.

Uncle Brim threw a pair of his boxers at the bed in frustration. Fuming, he looked at Junie's bag. The teenager was laying faceup on his bed, trying to imagine his future.

"What you got?" Uncle Brim demanded.

"Nothing."

The older man was already going through the young man's bag. He took out a box like the kind used for jewelry, felt-covered, only larger. "You got this. I can get something for this."

Junie snatched the box back. "No."

"This ain't no time for sentimentality, Junie. We're on the run, don't you understand?"

"Whose fault is that?"

"Junie." His uncle held his arms wide in an embracing gesture. "We're the only family the other has. We have to stick up for each other."

Junie was sitting up now. "Then how come I don't get half the money?"

Brim's eyes went agate and he reached back into his bag. The one item he wasn't considering pawning was the Glock Junie knew his uncle had packed. But was he about to put it upside his nephew's head?

What he pulled out instead was a deck of cards.

"We're sportin' men, let's play for it."

If he said no, would his uncle go crazy off? "Okay."

"None of that TV jive. Just straight-up Five Card Stud. You and me, youngster. Let's see who has the biggest ones."

Junie stood and his uncle handed him the deck. There was no desk, so the two marched into the small bathroom and Junie put the lid down on the toilet for a surface to shuffle the cards. Then they returned to the other room and stood at one of the twin beds.

The nephew dealt one down to each then back and forth, four to each player faceup. There was no bets, no bluffing, no tells. This was pure luck of the draw. His uncle had two queens and he had two deuces showing. They hesitated. A truck on the highway rattled the walls and blues singer Etta James' splendidly tortured voice seeped in from one of the nearby rooms. Each turned over their hole cards.

"I'll be damned," Brim hissed. "Trip twos beats my pair of ladies." He glared hard at his nephew.

"That's 'cause you rely on women too much," a female voice suddenly said.

An openmouthed Junie watched Missa walk in the unlocked door. She was dressed in hip-huggers, a black T-shirt and some fresh Air Jordans. She kissed Brim. "I drove Mama's car like you said," she told him.

"Good." Brim put the cards and his boxers away and zipped up his bag. He threw the keys to his Pontiac right on top of Junie's winning hand. "You rollin' with us?"

Junie considered what that meant. The next town, the next con or takedown. Always on the make, always one step ahead. "I'm straight."

"Go on with your bad self." Brim put an arm around Missa's waist and they started out. She stopped him.

"Give him his due, Brim. He didn't panic and didn't give up where you'd be. He did right."

Even though her kiss had been just a test, Junie liked her.

"We gonna need this money to stake us in our next action," Brim complained.

"Sign the pink to your car so he can at least sell that."

"I don't have it with me. And anyway, it ain't exactly legally in my name."

"He did right," she insisted.

Uncle Brim blew air through his puckered lips and counted out five hundred, but made it a thousand after the withering glare she laid on him. He handed it to Junie. "I'll see you around, huh?"

"Yeah."

On their way out, Missa gave Junie a wet smack on his cheek.

Junie sat on the bed and opened the box. In it was the bronze-colored medal his brother had been awarded in Iraq—posthumously, they'd called it. His name and rank was inscribed on the back of the thing. The white van with the two marines had pulled up to their apartment, and his mother had collapsed, right there on the porch. After that, though she'd been clean some five years, she got back on the pipe and as far as Junie knew, was still riding it hard. He shut the lid, tucked it in his bag, and left the motel room, buttoning up his jean jacket against the sudden chill.

Gary Phillips

Gary Phillips writes crime, mystery, and other sorts of stories in various mediums. He's working on a coming-of-age graphic novel; co-editing *The Darker Mask*, a collection of edgy superhero prose stories; and editing *Politics Noir*, an anthology of tawdry stories set in the most vicious arena there is. Alas, his experiences with poker inform him he's not an able player, but he just can't stay away from the chips and cards.

THE ROYAL COUPLE

by Mary Logue

"I got a tell on you, Kendra."

"Sure, Buddy," I baited him. I was helping him carry the poker table down the stairs to set it up in the basement. I had come over early to help him and his sister Shelley get ready to host the weekly Texas holdem poker tournament.

"No, you give yourself away."

"Really?" I acted disinterested.

"Yeah, you wiggle your pinkie finger

when you've got a good hand." He lifted his hand away from the poker table and showed me how I wiggled my finger.

I couldn't believe he told me my tell. What an idiot—a six-foot-tall idiot that I had a major crush on. But even as much as I liked him, I would never tell him that he scrunches his eyebrows together when he's got something good.

Buddy Walker was a senior at Mounds Park High. With dark brown hair that swung like a mop in his eyes, long eyelashes and a knockout smile, he was a handsome nerd, an unusual combination. What made him even more attractive was he didn't know how cute he was. He was the brother of my best friend, Shelley, which is how I got invited to join the Friday night poker game. Needless to say, I was the only girl in the game.

I'm a junior. I'm too smart for my own good, which makes me a bit of a geek. Boys tend to be intimidated by me. I'm okay-looking. Not great. I've got that long, thin, gangly look that some guys like. I haven't really had a boyfriend. I'm the kind of girl that guys like to hang out with, but don't usually ask out.

My main problem is I tell it like I see it. Guys don't always like that, I guess. I can't seem to help myself. If I know something I don't try to hide it and play dumb.

"Hey, Kendra, you doing anything tomorrow night?"

Buddy's question stopped me in my tracks. I was immediately suspicious. "Why d'you want to know?"

"I was just wondering."

"Why?"

"You want to do something?" Buddy asked me.

I just about dropped my side of the poker table. "Tomorrow night?" Why did I repeat that? "I think so . . . sure . . ."

"Great. Put those legs down," Buddy instructed as we started to set up the poker table.

Buddy had just asked me out. I had been playing poker with him for two months hoping this would happen. I'd been studying the game, trying to learn the chances of getting a pair, a flush, a royal flush. One in something like 30,000. I figured that was just about the same as the chance of Buddy asking me out. But I had hit the big one. The nuts. A date with Buddy. Tomorrow night. I wanted to jump up and down and scream. I wanted to instant message my five closest friends.

Instead, I put the legs down on the poker table.

"I'm feeling lucky tonight," Buddy told me.

I felt beyond lucky. Now I might never have to play poker again. I had enjoyed learning to play the game, but I just wasn't much of a gambler. I didn't like to lose my money and had never believed in luck. Games like chess, bridge, or even Scrabble, which involved more skill, were more my style. In the long run, poker was about skill, but in the short term, like one night of playing, it was way too much about luck.

Shelley came clomping down the stairs with a big bowl of popcorn. Instead of poker, she played housewife. She made all the treats, deejayed the music, freshened beverages, and generally made herself useful. Since she was going out with Ted, one of the other players, she would hang over his shoulder and watch the game.

I wanted to tell her that Buddy had asked me out, so I dashed up the stairs, hoping she'd follow me. She didn't.

So I went to the bathroom, closed the door, and looked at myself in the mirror. I looked the same as I had at home: blue eyes a little too far apart, light brown hair pulled up in a loose knot, jeans hanging off my hips, chipped nail polish, lightly smeared eye makeup, a tight purple T-shirt. I lifted up my hand and wiggled my pinkie finger. Tonight, luck was my friend.

I found Shelley downstairs in the bar area making chip dip. A must for a poker party as far as I was concerned. Buddy was not too far away.

I mouthed, "Your brother asked me out."

"What?"

I whispered it again.

She gave me a crooked look and said, "What are you whispering about? I can't hear you."

I took out my phone and punched in the message. She took out hers and read it. We high-fived and tore open a bag of Cheetos.

The doorbell rang. She handed me the Cheetos to put in a bowl as Ted walked down the stairs. He leaned over to kiss her and she stuffed a Cheeto in his mouth. I left the two of them alone.

When I sidled up to the table, Buddy was getting out the poker chips, setting them in stacks for each of the players.

The way this Friday night holdem game worked is we each put in twenty bucks and got a thousand dollars in chips. Whoever was left standing at the end of the night won all the money. In two months of playing I had never won. But two weeks ago I had come close. I was getting better. Watching the tournaments on TV and reading a few poker books had helped my game.

"Who's all coming tonight?" I asked. "Besides Ted."

"Weinie, Jeff and Bartleby."

"That's all?"

"Yeah. Franko had to go out of town with his folks. Trent is incarcerated."

"What? What'd he do this time?"

"Took his mom's car without asking in the middle of the night and ran a stoplight, then hit a cop car."

"Wow."

"He knows how to do it."

I sat down and fingered my chips. "I'm going to miss Franko."

Buddy nodded. "He gives away his money pretty easily."

"Mainly to you."

Buddy had won last time. Weinie the two times before that and then Buddy again. Bartleby wasn't a bad player, he just couldn't bluff and he couldn't go for the kill. He'd back off of a good hand. Jeff was a very tight player, which meant he never lost too soon, but he never won. Two weeks ago, I had come close to winning against Weinie, but then I had lost to him in a bad beat.

I think bad beat stories are pathetic—except if a bad beat happens to me. I had two queens in my hand and got another on the flop. I went all-in. I was ready to win. Then the last two cards rained down two spades and Weinie beat me with a spade flush. I know it's the rules but I don't think a measly spade flush should beat a set of queens. They just looked so pretty, my three queens.

I lined up my chips and realized I didn't really care what happened tonight. I had already won the game I was really playing. I looked over at Buddy; he glanced up at me and smiled his megawatt smile. Ted and Shelley tromped down the stairs with Weinie in tow. Jeff and Bartleby showed up a few minutes later. They sat on either side of me.

Bartleby punched me in the arm. "This is my night. I've got the power."

I thought of punching him back, but decided not to waste my energy. "Whatever," I said.

When I first started playing with these guys, they treated me like a girl. They teased me and pestered me. But now they just treated me like one of the guys. I think they respected that I had stuck it out.

The night went by fast. Before, I had always cared how I played. Now it just wasn't that important to me. No matter what happened Buddy and I were going out tomorrow night. I didn't have to prove anything. So I played a little wilder than usual and I think it took the boys by surprise. They let me have hands they shouldn't have.

By midnight, it was down to Weinie, Buddy and me. Weinie had the fewest chips. I figured he was sitting on maybe a thousand. Buddy and I split the remaining five thousand, but my pile was maybe a little bigger.

Then Buddy and Weinie got into a hand. With just a deuce and an eight, I folded immediately. The flop came three of hearts, five of clubs and a jack of diamonds. Both Buddy and Weinie checked. The next card was an ace of spades. Weinie liked it. I could tell because he peeked at his cards twice. I knew he had at least one ace. I was sure that Buddy knew it too. Buddy's eyebrows quivered as he matched the bet. The last card came— another five. Weinie went all-in. Buddy thought about it for a few moments. Or maybe he wasn't thinking about it. I think he was just savoring the moment. Then he pushed all his chips in too.

Weinie laid down his cards quickly. An ace and a jack. Buddy took his time. First he laid down his ace. Weinie reached for the chips. Then Buddy laid down his five. Weinie groaned, slapped his forehead and stood up.

"You're one lucky dude."

"That's what I am indeed." Buddy raked all the chips over. Now he had slightly more chips than I had.

It was just the two of us left. I had never battled it out head-to-head with Buddy before. It wasn't exactly the way I wanted this game to end. I felt like just giving him the next hand or two to get it over with, but I'd wait and see what kind of cards I got. I probably wouldn't have any choice in the matter.

I got dealt the king and queen of hearts. I knew that a king-queen combo wasn't the best hand, but when it was down to two players such a hand gained in strength. Anyway, I felt like staying in. I liked my handsome couple. I saw it as a sign—the royal couple of hearts.

Buddy bet $500. I called.

Weinie flipped over the first card of the flop: ten of hearts. Then an ace of spades followed and a three of diamonds.

I liked the ten even though it wouldn't immediately do me any good, but maybe I'd get some kind of flush. And if a jack came, I'd have a straight.

Buddy scrunched his eyebrows and raised a thousand. His actions made me pretty sure he had an ace in his hand. I almost threw my hand in, but I was ready for this game to be over. I'd play it out, then let Buddy have it. I called.

The card on the turn was the ace of hearts. Buddy loved it. He was trying to play it cool, but his eyebrows had become butterflies, almost lifting off his forehead. He pushed in his pile of chips. I figured he had me beat—at least one ace in his hand, possibly two. I had a draw to a flush, or a straight, or even a royal flush—but he was a big favorite. I went all-in, ready to give the game to him.

Buddy showed four aces. Then he looked at me to show my hand.

I shook my head. "Not yet. There's one more card."

Weinie looked at both of us and turned up the final card. I stopped breathing. It was the one card in the deck that could beat quad aces, the ultimate gutshot: the jack of hearts. And what a knave he was, smiling up at me.

Feeling my little finger wanting to wiggle, I put my hands in my lap and stared at the board. Impossible. A royal flush. A hand like this doesn't happen. Not in just two months of playing poker. Not in two years of playing poker.

The queen stared at the king. She gave him the once-over. She knew that if she let him win this hand, their date tomorrow night would be much better. He would have more money. He would be feeling great.

When I glanced over at Buddy I could tell he was trying to read me. What was funny was that I knew he had no idea what kind of hand I was holding. With this hand, at this point in the game, I shouldn't have to think twice about what to do. With the hand I was holding, there was only one thing to do.

I looked again at the queen, staring at the king. It came down to the dilemma smart women face again and again—should you beat the man you love?

My beautiful hand. The whole royal court of hearts. One in 30,000. I would never in my life get this hand again. Of that I was certain.

Buddy was trying not to smile. He thought he had it made. My pinkie finger was holding steady. I wanted to laugh.

I could quietly fold my hand, shove it into the deck of cards so no one could see what I had.

Or I could introduce the royal couple to the world.

I lifted up my cards.

It was going to be tough choice.

Mary Logue

Award-winning poet and mystery writer Mary Logue was born and raised in Minnesota and knows more about bridge than she does about poker. Her most recent books are *Snatched* and *Skullduggery*, middle-grade mysteries she wrote with Pete Hautman; *Poison Heart,* her seventh crime novel; and *Meticulous Attachment,* her third book of poems. She has also published a young adult novel, *Dancing with an Alien.* She lives with Pete Hautman in Minnesota and Wisconsin and watches him play poker online for hours on end.

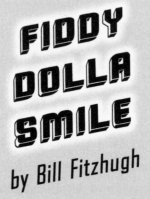

FIDDY DOLLA SMILE

by Bill Fitzhugh

The whole thing was Corey's idea, but he needed a partner. Somebody he trusted. Somebody no one else knew. That's where Adam came in. He went to a different school.

They were sitting in Corey's car that night, parked in front of Tyler Brandon's house, waiting.

Adam said, "Sort of like Robin Hood?"

"Sort of," Corey replied. "Or the Lone Ranger."

"What's that make me?"

"Tonto, I guess. Or Little John. Your pick."

"I'll take Little John," Adam said. "So that makes her, what, Maid Marian?"

Corey smiled, just thinking about the first time he saw Melissa's big green eyes, passing him in the hall at the start of school. She didn't notice him and he was too shy to say anything. So he worshipped her from afar and thought, maybe someday.

But then Corey heard some ugly rumors. Rumors about what Tyler Brandon had done to Melissa. Roofies was what Corey heard. Date rape, they said. Drug-facilitated sexual assault. She told somebody at school and all hell broke loose. But Tyler's dad and some influential alums applied some pressure and the whole thing got swept under the rug amidst a lot of winking and the men talking about how boys will be boys. And it wasn't the first thing Tyler got away with, or the last.

Melissa switched schools and Corey hadn't seen her since. Figured he might never see her again. Figured she'd carry that scar for a long time. None of it was right.

After Corey heard all the stories, something strange happened. He felt an obligation to do something about it, to defend Melissa's honor or something, like out of a damn storybook.

Adam said, "I'm ready whenever you are."

That summer, there was a game every Saturday night over at Tyler's house, a McMansion in a gated community out in the sprawl. A white-bread ghetto where the air was sick with the sweet smell of too much fabric softener.

Tyler's parents were usually there, but they stayed upstairs, out of the way, listening to Faith Hill or somebody like that. They didn't seem to care what went on as long as nothing got broken and the cops didn't show.

Tyler and his friends had been playing poker together since junior high. Tyler was at the center of this universe. The starting quarterback, he was going to win them state this year, or so everybody said. His friends called him L. K., which stood for Lady Killa, he even had *El Kay* inked on his arm in case anybody had any questions. Tyler cultivated a rep for having his way with the girls. Never mind those rumors about roofies. "Nobody ever proved a thing," he sneered. "Never even went to court."

His crew included Derek, Justin, Ian, Zach, Matt, and Ryan. They'd all be seniors at Dillard High in the fall. They all played football and they all had nicknames: Speedo, Phatts, Grilla, Slyce, Z-Unit, and Dark Meat.

They weren't always seven deep at the table—like that time Z-Unit was in the hospital after doing those bogus steroids (those big-ass biceps of his bulging like a honeydew). But there was usually somebody else to sit in. Everybody at school knew the game was going on because it had been going on for years, so they'd drop by, hang.

They didn't bother with a button or blinds, big or small. Deal rotated and dealer anted for everybody. Aces went both ways. Cards spoke. No limit on the betting.

Speedo tossed a queen on the board, saying, "It's a mop-squeezer on the river."

They'd been playing for an hour with just five. Some girls were hanging in the kitchen, drinking beer, didn't want to play.

"Yo, dog, turn that up!" Justin was moving to one of Pimp C's chopped and screwed beats, shoulders rolling, head counterbalancing his torso's movements. "Yo, Tyler," Justin said, gang-gesturing across the table. " 'Sup?" Justin had thrown down a pair of eights and was waiting for Tyler to show his hand. "You 'bout it or what?"

"Shit, nigga, whatchoo thank?" Tyler spanked his cards onto the table. "Booya, beyatch! San Francisco busboy in the howse!" His two pair beat Justin's eights.

The others howled and hooted and bumped fists. Grilla pointed at the cards, shaking his head. "What's a San Francisco busboy?"

Tyler stacked his chips and said, "Yo, it's a queen with a tray. Do the math."

A second later Phatts leaned back, holding his hands out. "A yo trip, I needs a sip. Who's got the lean?"

"Yo, who you thank?" Tyler slipped a medicine bottle from his pocket and wiggled it for all to see. He'd hooked up with somebody at a hospital who was jacking the supply room for the codeine-laced cough syrup. He'd been dealing for months. Cheese was flowin' in—he had a couple grand in a cigar box.

Phatts, Grilla, and Slyce chipped in to make the buy. Phatts leaned back in his chair and yelled toward the kitchen, "Yo, we need some ice up in this bitch. Crushed!"

Ten minutes later the side door slid open and three girls sauntered in like a parade on a tight budget. Teresa, Keira, and Haley.

Tyler pointed at them one at a time. "Ho, ho, ho! And it ain't even Christmas." He looked to his boys for approval.

Phatts gave him a laugh and a "No diggity!"

Everybody cracked up and Speedo said, "El Kay, you are one trill-ass nigga."

Haley rolled her eyes. "Would you shut *up*? You guys are about as black as Nicole Richie."

"Not even," Keira said. "I mean I think she's, like, at least, I dunno, like a little black or what*ever*." She rolled her eyes and headed for the kitchen.

Corey and Adam got out of the car. They stood on the sidewalk for a moment as Adam slipped something into his mouth. He turned to Corey and said, "You like my smile?" He grinned like a chimp who'd eaten a mirror ball.

Corey laughed when he saw it. He said, "That cracks me up every time."

"That's good."

Corey said, "You remember all the signals?"

"Prolly."

"Probably?"

"No, definitely."

"Good. You sure you want to do this?"

"Anything for Maid Marian."

Corey had been to poker night at Tyler's twice before. Once at a big party where he just kind of blended in, observing their rituals more than participating. The other time, he played some cards. He lost twenty but it had been worth it just to see them up close, acting the way they did. Like they had no idea who they were and if they put on a big enough act, maybe they wouldn't have to find out.

Tyler seemed to think Corey was okay, which made him

okay with the others. There was no telling how they'd react to Adam, though.

Slyce was about to deal the flop when the side door slid open again. Phatts hid the syrup as Corey stepped in.

"Yo! Fresh meat!" Slyce said.

"Hope you brought some scrilla, dilla." Tyler rubbed his thumb against his fingers.

Phatts pulled his bottle back out and poured the syrup over cracked ice.

Corey played it cool, giving a slight upward nod. " 'Sup, fellas?"

"You gonna shut the door or what?" Tyler held his hands out for an answer.

Corey looked outside and gave a little sideways gesture with his head. A second later, Adam slipped into the room with a goofy, dim expression. "This is my friend Adam," Corey said. "We were driving around, decided to stop in, you know, check the game."

The guys gave Adam the twice-over. There was something weird about the look on his face. Finally, Grilla looked at Corey and said, "Yo, what's with your whodi?"

Corey looked at Adam, then back at the guys with a shrug. "Just kinda quiet."

Slyce put his index fingers to his temples. "Is he, like, a 'tard or something?"

"Hey." Adam looked over Corey's shoulder. "I'm standing right here."

"So for sure you're not deaf then," Tyler said.

"For sure."

.¥And obviously your mouth works."

"Sure does." That's when Adam stepped out from behind Corey and flashed his smile. It looked like a jewelry store with healthy gums and what appeared to be three thousand dollars' worth of platinum and diamond mouth-bling.

"Dayum!" Slyce couldn't believe his eyes. "Check this nigga's grille!"

Slyce, Phatts, and Speedo jumped up for a closer look.

Slyce said, "Dogg's frontin' some serious ice-caps."

The girls came in from the kitchen to see what all the shouting was about. Keira said, "That's the bling all right."

A-D-A-M was spelled out across his front teeth in princess-cut diamonds set in platinum shiny as a new set of chrome spinners.

Corey tried to act like it was no big thing but it felt like setting a hook in a fish's mouth. A gaudy set of orthodontics had elevated Adam from retard to playa like flipping a switch.

"Yo, where'd you *get* that?" Speedo wanted to know.

"His parents," Corey said. "They own a chain of jewelry stores that make those."

"Won't let me get them permanent though," Adam said. "This's like a retainer." He reached for his mouth. "See?" He took them out but nobody actually wanted to touch the things. Adam shrugged, put them back in his mouth.

Tyler didn't like the way everybody's attention had shifted. He said, "Yo, Speedo, you gon' floss the bitch or what? Sit down." Then he turned to Corey. "You playin'?"

"Sure."

"Buy-in's forty."

Corey dropped two twenties, got his chips, and sat between Phatts and Slyce.

"Hey," Adam said, patting his pocket. "I got money."

"I bet you do," Phatts replied, wishing his own parents gave him everything he wanted.

Corey nodded toward the kitchen. "Why don't you give the girls another look at your grille?"

Adam shrugged and said, "Yeah, all right."

Tyler said to Corey, "What are you, like, his babysitter?"

Corey shook his head but didn't make too big deal out of it—he wanted to play it just right. Wanted Tyler to extended the invitation. "No, I just don't think he oughta be swimming with the sharks is all." He made a little face that suggested remedial reading or something.

"You said he wasn't a 'tard."

"He's not but . . ." A little shrug to put the scent in the water.

Tyler smelled it. He leaned back and said, "Yo, Retardo Montalban, you wanna play?"

Adam cracked a goofy smile and said, "Fo shizzle!"

This guy was already getting under Tyler's skin, irritating him like somebody telling him no. He poured more syrup and took a sip. "Buy-in's forty."

Boom. L'il Flip came on the stereo, thumping out of the speakers like a loud hypnotist. Boom. The guys kept sippin' the syrup, getting higher with each one. Boom. Tyler and his posse played on in a woozy blur. Boom. Corey tried not to smile too much.

Boom. He felt like Robin Hood about to do his heroic deed of valor. Boom.

The girls gyrated out of the kitchen, gravitating toward Adam, treating him like a cute pet with funny teeth. He sponged it up, played court jester, the posse's motley fool, like he didn't know a pair of aces from a pair of shoes.

The whole scene was working every nerve in Tyler's brain. He got agitated and cracked another bottle of syrup. He wasn't embalmed yet but he could get there quick from where he was.

Perfect, Corey thought. *Makes things that much easier.* They wouldn't need fancy mechanics with these guys. No marked cards or any of that. All they needed was in Adam's smile.

Slyce was getting good cards and making the most of it until somebody passed him a blunt; then he started laying crazy bets and bluffs you couldn't pull on a first grader. Three hands later, he was toast.

Nobody seemed to think anything about the way Adam kept worrying the letters on his teeth with his tongue, figured it was a nervous tic or that the retainer felt funny, like having a sliver of corn husk between two molars. But each touch meant something if you knew how to read it, like Corey did.

After Phatts and Grilla went back into their pockets for another forty each, there was three hundred and sixty bucks in the game, which wasn't bad. It was a start. But Corey and Adam had come to teach a more expensive lesson.

Next hand the flop was four, nine, jack, all clubs. Grilla bet thirty. Adam figured him for three jacks and saw an opportunity to test his theory on Tyler's tell. So he signaled Corey by touching the "M" tooth and sliding his tongue away from the rest of the letters. If Corey liked his hand, he'd stay, otherwise he knew to fold, which is what he did.

Tyler stopped rolling his shoulders and laid a big bet. Grilla called. The turn was a ten of hearts. Didn't help anybody. Tyler sat still and bet some more. Grilla stayed with him. The river was the ace of clubs and all of a sudden, Tyler started groovin' to the beat again. Grilla bet his trips jacks, Tyler raised, and won with a flush.

Adam looked at Corey, who nodded that he'd seen the tell, that Tyler danced with good cards and was paralyzed by his bluffs. Now they'd want to watch him for a little while, just to be sure, before they went for the kill.

A while later Speedo pushed in the last of his chips. Phatts stayed with him.

Adam signaled Corey again. They both folded, since neither of them had anything and now they both knew it. Best to let Speedo and Phatts fight one another.

"Motown," Speedo said. Jacks and fives.

"Shiiiit." Phatts shook his head. "Jackson Five ain't nevva sang no song good enough to beat trips nines, beyatch."

With Speedo gone, it was three down, one to go.

A few hands later, Tyler bailed before the flop, leaving Phatts stuck between Corey and Adam. Adam touched the first "A" with his tongue, the signal to whipsaw the poor sucker until he was all-in. Then Corey docked a full boat, leaving Phatts wondering why the hell he'd bet on a ten-high straight.

By one in the morning, it was down to Tyler, Corey, and Adam. Tyler was foggy from the syrup but he was too macho to call it a night.

Adam and Corey figured it was time to set the table for the endgame. So, for the next half hour, Tyler won every single time he tried a bluff. It fed his sense of superiority, blinded him from the possibility he could be conned. He was just better than everybody else.

A couple of hands later, Corey tossed his last ten bucks' worth of chips to Adam and said, "I'm done, fellas." Their collusion was designed to get them to this point while they figured Tyler's tell. Now, Corey could sit back and watch that smug son of a bitch get schooled. Bad enough what he'd done to Melissa, but to brag about it? Acting like he was untouchable? This was going to be fun.

Tyler looked at his watch. It was nearly two. " 'Bout time to wrap this bitch up," he said, glancing at Adam's chips. "And it shouldn't take long."

Phatts dealt the hand.

Adam checked his hole cards then smiled and did something with his tongue that told Corey he was holding ace-king suited. Just keeping him informed. Keira and Haley were sitting on either side of Adam, like mascots on the arms of his chair.

Tyler sipped his syrup, checked his hole cards, and kept moving with the music. "Let's get this over with," he said, tossing in a stack of ten five-dollar chips. "Fiddy."

Adam knew it was still early, that a lot could happen on the flop. But with ace-king suited, he liked his odds. He glanced at Corey, saw the dreamy look in his eyes that he got whenever he was thinking about Melissa. Adam snapped his shiny teeth and said, "Okay, fiddy, fo shizzle!"

Keira and Haley laughed and rubbed Adam's head for luck.

Tyler couldn't believe he'd invited this retard to play cards, let alone that it had come down to the two of them. He told Phatts to hurry up and deal. "Shorty here's gettin' on my nerves."

Phatts dealt the flop.

"Seven, queen, ace, suited up—all diamonds," he said.

Haley pointed at the cards saying, "Diamonds are a girl's best friend."

"Yo! Yo! Yo! That's what I'm talkin' 'bout!" Tyler held his hole cards to his nose, sniffing. "Yo, smells like wedding rings, know what I'm sayin'?" Boom. The bass was thumping. Boom. Tyler was still moving to the beat, but not as much. He said, "I already gots the nut flush, Shorty. You ought just go on and fold right now." Boom.

Adam flashed his goofy smile and considered the flop. The diamonds didn't help, though he did pair his aces. Problem was, he couldn't read Tyler. He still seemed to be moving to the beat a little, just not as much as before. Were they wrong about his tell? Had he been setting them up? Was he so crunked on the syrup that the system had stopped working?

All Tyler needed was a diamond or two in his pocket. If he didn't have it yet, he still had two more shots. And if he *got* the flush, Adam would need an ace or a king on both the turn *and* the river. Long odds there. Still, Adam figured heroic deeds always involved some risk. He bet thirty.

Tyler didn't hesitate. He said, "See that and raise fiddy."

"Tyler!" Haley clucked her tongue and said, "Don't be such a bully."

Tyler dismissed her with a sneer. "Problem is, nobody axed you."

Adam leaned back so he could get his hand into his pocket. He pulled some more cash and called. He looked like a lamb being led to slaughter.

Phatts dealt the turn. "King of clubs. No help on the flush."

"Who needs help?" Tyler said, rubbing his hole cards together like he was trying to start a fire. "I already gots my own diamond mine."

Phatts pointed at Tyler. "Bet's to you, El Kay."

Tyler grinned and sent chips flying. "Flush says fiddy more."

Boom. The king gave Adam two pair. He knew he'd need help on the river to beat a flush. Boom. He couldn't tell for sure if Tyler was swaying from too much syrup or if he was moving to the music. Boom. One way to find out. Boom. Adam said, "Call."

Phatts dealt the river. "Two of diamonds."

Slyce said, "Who's got the flush?"

Tyler thumped his chest. "Just call me Mr. DeBeers, yo."

"Your bet."

Tyler figured there was only one way to handle it. No way he was going to lose to a retard in front of his crew. He grew still as a casket and said, "I'm all-in." He pushed his pile to the middle of the table.

Phatts counted it and said, "Three seventy-five."

"And before you start thinking about it," Tyler said. "I ain't done." He turned to Speedo and said, "Yo, watch my cards. I'll be right back." Tyler left the room and returned with his cigar box. His syrup money. He counted out another six twenty-five, dropped it in the pot. "A thousand even." Tyler figured that was enough to scare him off.

Adam reached up and took out his grille. "This is worth about two thousand."

Corey got wide-eyed like somebody had drawn a gun on him. "Are you crazy? Your dad'll kill you. Don't do it."

Tyler was stuck. He couldn't fold now and surrender to this re-tard. He'd never live that down. He could think of only one thing to do. He reached back into his cigar box and said, "Call."

Boom. Nobody could believe it, least of all Tyler. The girls were slack jawed. Boom. The posse was nervous. Boom.

Slyce said, "Showtime!"

Speedo said, "No, toilet time! Show him the flush, El Kay!"

Boom. But nobody made a move to show anything.

Boom. "Let's see some cards!"

Adam tossed his big slick on the table. Boom. "Two pair," he said. "Aces and kings."

Boom. The posse erupted, hooting like a cage of monkeys.

Boom. Haley started to rub Adam's back out of sympathy.

Boom. "What're you waitin' on, El Kay, flush that bitch."

Boom. But Tyler just sat there. No more swagger, no more beyatches, no nothing. He just sat there. Boom. Perfectly still. Like a girl all drugged up. Boom.

After a few seconds, Phatts reached over and flipped Tyler's hole cards. Seven and nine of clubs.

Slyce said, "Pair of sevens?"

As they walked to the car Adam said, "What're you going to do with your half?"

"Think I might ask Melissa out."

"For a date?"

"A real expensive date," Corey said.

"Good man."

Corey pulled the car from the curb, smiling, and said, "And I mean, really expensive."

"So, when did you know?"

"I wasn't sure until the river," Corey said.

"That's because you're blinded by love," Adam said, mocking him with kissy noises. He said, "I had him pegged after the flop."

Corey punched him in the arm, said, "Bullshit."

"No diggity." Adam smiled and took out the grille. "I was scared shitless until he threw in all his money. Then all of a sudden it looked like he'd suffered a spinal cord injury."

"Yeah, he did stiffen up a bit." Corey gestured at the grille and said, "Where'd you get that thing anyway?"

"eBay," Adam said. "Forty-nine ninety-five."

"Used?"

"Prolly."

Bill Fitzhugh

Bill Fitzhugh is the award-winning writer of seven satiric crime novels, including *Pest Control, Heart Seizure,* and *Highway 61 Resurfaced. The New York Times* called him "a strange and deadly amalgam of screenwriter and comic novelist [whose] facility and wit, and taste for the perverse, put him in a league with Carl Hiaasen and Elmore Leonard." He does a weekly show on XM Satellite Radio called *Fitzhugh's All Hand Mixed Vinyl.* He grew up in Mississippi playing poker with his brothers and their friends, and still remembers the night he drew to an inside straight flush. He lives in Los Angeles with his wife, three big dogs, and a cat named Crusty Boogers.

SUICIDE KING

by Walter Sorrells

"I'm going to kill myself tomorrow." I threw a dime in the pot.

"You're bluffing again, Mark," Ray said to me. He kicked in a dime, called my bet. We were playing Five Card Draw, one-eyed jacks and suicide kings wild. "It's right there on your face."

"Believe what you want," I said. I looked at my cards. I had totally nada. I debated folding. But I hate folding. It makes me feel like a weakling, a loser. "Maybe not tomorrow. But Saturday at the latest. Tomorrow, I've got yearbook staff after school, so I won't have time. But, yeah, Saturday, definitely—good-bye, cruel world."

Eleanor, my ex-girlfriend, called. The dimes made a thin clink on the table.

Justin and Benjy folded. I raised a dime.

Ray was like, "Pffffff!" He threw in his dime without a second's hesitation.

I was like, "What, you don't think I've got the balls?"

"I don't think you've got the cards."

I was talking about killing myself and he was still all caught up in this dumb card game.

I drew three. Which is pretty much admitting you don't have squat. One of my cards was the king of hearts, the suicide king, the one that looks like he's sticking a sword in his head. Wild card. Still, with the crap cards in my hand, all it gave me was a pair of eights. Three wild cards in the game, that was worse than nothing.

Ray gave me the level look, like—*What?* And I felt all twisted up inside. Ray hadn't drawn any cards. Either he was bluffing or he had my ass beat. And suddenly I just felt like I couldn't go through with it.

I could feel a twitch in one eyelid and a stiffness in my face. I probably looked like a giant neon sign was wired to my head, flashing LOSER LOSER LOSER LOSER. I knew Ray could see it.

"All-in," I said, pushing my little heap of coins into the middle.

"Quit being a moron," Ray said. "This isn't no limit. Dime limit, dude. Dime! In or out?"

I looked around the table. Eleanor was avoiding my eyes. Justin shrugged. Benjy was like, "Ray's house, Ray's rules. Dime limit."

I threw my cards down, swept the coins off the table—my coins, the pot, everything. They went spanging around all over the floor of Ray's basement.

I walked out.

I could hear Justin's voice as I stomped up the steps. "What's *his* problem?"

Ray was like, "You call his bluff, he gets all wuss on you. Same as always."

When I got home my mom and dad were asleep. I walked quietly into my old man's study, opened the lock on his display case and pulled out the Luger my granddad brought back from Germany after World War II. It has the name of some dead kraut engraved on the side. Supposedly my granddad killed the guy during the Battle of the Bulge. That's the story he tells, anyway. But then everybody in my family is a bunch of liars, so it's hard to know.

I cocked the empty gun, put the barrel in my mouth, pulled the trigger. It wasn't loaded or anything. I know because I checked. Only a total idiot handles a gun without checking to make sure it's not loaded. I decided to practice how I would do it if I was really going to off myself.

Cock the gun, open my mouth, stick it in, pull the trigger. Cock, open, in, click. Cock, open, in, click. The metal has a sour taste.

I used to really like playing poker. We'd go over to Justin's and joke around and fart and stuff, and I'd lose a shitload or I'd win a shitload. One thing about me, I never end up in the middle. I bet hard, whether I'm bluffing or not. If you're gonna go down, go down in flames, right?

Cock, open, in, click.

About eight weeks ago, though, my girlfriend Eleanor—well, like I said, now she's my *ex*-girlfriend—asked if she could play. I was like, "Fine."

But it wasn't the same after that. The minute she walked in the door that first time, I started losing. I haven't won squat since she showed up. Somehow she always knows if I'm bullshitting. And Ray picked up on it. I don't know if she told him what to look for, but after that there was something that he could see in my face. And so now I'm down like a hundred bucks to Ray. And it's all Eleanor's fault.

Plus, after like three weeks, Eleanor gave me this speech, about how "Let's be friends, blah blah blah, blah blah blah, blah blah blah," all that crap. The big blow-off. And I'm like, "Whatever. Mindy Edison asked me for a date last week anyway. Maybe I'll just go out with her." Mindy Edison is this cheerleader who probably wouldn't talk to me for a million dollars.

Then Eleanor was like, "You're not gonna get a bug up your ass if I keep coming to poker are you?"

Well, what am I gonna do? I have to act like I'm cool with it. So I was all: "Yeah, whatever. Maybe I'll bring Mindy Edison. She's better-looking than you anyway."

Cock, open, in, click.

Then last week I saw Ray and Eleanor at the movies together. They're like, "Hey, dude, what's up." Acting like they're just hanging out. But I knew different. I'm not stupid.

Cock, open, in, click.

As I was pulling the trigger, my dad walked in. "What in the name of creation are you doing, Mark?" He grabbed the gun then started dope-slapping me in the head, messing up my hair.

In my yearbook staff meeting the next day I told everybody that I'd written this short story and it had been accepted by *The New Yorker*. Mr. Gilliland, the sponsor of the yearbook, was like, "Really! That's extraordinary news!" Mr. Gilliland is this Earth Science teacher whose tongue kind of hangs out of his mouth when he's thinking. He's the most gullible dude I've ever met in my life. I told him once that my old man was an astronaut. Ever since then, every time the Earth Science book talked about meteorites or planets or any of that junk, he'd always tells the class how my dad flew on the space shuttle.

"Yeah," I said, "it's about this kid who plays poker. He's like this genius poker player and he goes to the poker world series in Las Vegas and everything."

All the kids were just rolling their eyes.

"I did *not* know they had a World Series of Poker!" Mr. Gilliland said. "Fascinating!"

Later I was fooling around on the computer, laying out the part of the yearbook with all the athletics in it. I was modifying the pictures in Photoshop so that all the girls on the volleyball team looked like they had male equipment in their pants. I did it kind of subtly so that nobody would notice until after it was printed. All except Eleanor. I gave her this great big bulge, so she looked hung like a horse.

Eleanor came up and said, "Very funny, Mark. Mr. Gilliland will kill you if he sees that."

"Won't matter," I said. "I'll be dead by then."

"Is this about me and Ray?" she said. "All this suicide crap?"

"I could care less about you and Ray."

"You are such a liar, Mark. Just be honest for once."

"Believe what you want to," I said. "After I'm dead? If you want to believe it's your fault and feel all guilty for being a back-stabbing traitor—hey, that's your problem."

"If you don't take that disgusting thing out of my picture," she said, "I'm telling Mr. Gilliland." She leaned forward and squinted at the screen. I could smell her, the smell of her deodor-ant. Is it totally gay that I get all weak in the knees when I smell Lady Speed Stick? "You could make my boobs look a little bigger, though," she said.

I went home and started writing this story, for real. I don't know why. I've never written a short story before. Turns out it's easy. Any idiot could do it. The kid's name in the story is Rex Master-man, and he's this really smooth guy who wears sunglasses and plays poker. In the story he's so good at poker that other kids won't play him anymore, so he gets in this Texas Holdem game with all these grown-ups. At the end of the story, he wins this restaurant from this big card player.

After I was done, I thought about it and remembered that I

had read that same ending in some dumb book once. But who's gonna notice?

Just to make sure nobody might think I ripped off the idea, I add this part where the guy who lost the restaurant tries to fight Rex Masterman, but Rex knows Brazilian jujitsu, and Rex beats this guy up and throws him in this swimming pool next door to the restaurant, and there's this totally hot chick lying there on a beach chair watching the fight while she sunbathes in this very tiny thong bikini. The way I describe her, she looks exactly like Mindy Edison, the cheerleader I mentioned earlier. Same red hair, same china blue eyes, same fabulous rack. When the fight's over, this hot babe looks at Rex and says, "That was the coolest thing I ever saw in my life."

And Rex looks at her through his sunglasses and goes, "That's what they all say."

And then he just walks off and leaves her lying there, looking at him with this really disappointed look on her face. Not even bothering to talk to her, he's that cool.

Which is the end of the story.

We had a poker game on Saturday.

"Thought you were gonna kill yourself today, Mark," Ray said as he was dealing the first game.

"I'm waiting till after I get done winning all your money to-night," I said.

He went, "Yeah right."

"What are we playing?" Benjy said.

"Seven Card Stud," Ray said. "Suicide kings and one-eyed jacks wild."

Ray loves all these dopey wild card games. He told me once that he memorized the odds for every conceivable wild card game. If it was me, he'd have been lying. But knowing Ray, it could be true.

"Yeah," I said. "I was thinking about killing myself by sticking a sword through my head. Like the suicide king? But now I'm thinking I'll just eat the trusty old nine millimeter."

Eleanor slammed her fist on the table. "Could you *please* shut up with that suicide crap, Mark? You're really pissing me off."

I was like, "Excuse *me* if my life sucks so bad that I feel like ending my suffering."

My up card was a ten of hearts. I picked up my first down card. Jack of spades. A wild card. Nice. I looked at the next card. I couldn't believe it. I mean, I could *not* believe it. It was the suicide king. I had two of the three wild cards. I was going to totally rip Ray a new one. Next was a queen of hearts. Man, oh man!

"Your bet, Mark," Ray said.

I scratched my head and kind of sighed, trying to act like I had iffy cards. I put the tip of my finger on a nickel, hesitated, then pushed it out.

"Look at this performance," Ray said.

"Fold," Benjy said.

"Fold," Justin said.

"Fold," Eleanor said.

I looked at Ray. "Go ahead," I said. "Be a sissy. Fold."

He put his finger on a nickel then a dime, like he was going to see me and raise me. But then he went, "Psych!"

And he pulled back the money and tossed his cards into the middle, making them spin around real fast.

"You're all assholes!" I said.

"What?" Ray said. "You had the suicide king didn't you? Probably had one of the jacks, too. Huh? Am I right?"

I put the cards down so they couldn't see them, so they couldn't see that Ray had read the whole thing exactly.

"It's right there on your face," he said.

"You're all gonna be sorry when I'm dead," I said.

My dad had locked up the Luger somewhere, so I couldn't get at it. But that was okay. Who needs a gun? I had seen in this samurai flick about how they commit hara kiri in Japan when they want to go out with honor, all the technical things involved in it. So I went in the kitchen and got a boning knife that Mom uses for cutting meat off chickens and stuff.

The samurai dude in the movie took this really scalding bath and then he dressed in this beautiful, spotless white outfit. Next he wrote this super-short poem about the reflection of the moon on the surface of a still pond or something. Then he sat down on the floor and pulled his shirt off so his upper body was bare. His muscles were all ripply and shiny, the skin red from the hot bath. Then he wrapped a perfectly white piece of cloth around the handle of the blade so that only about two inches of razor-sharp steel was sticking out. He took a deep, slow breath—all calm, his face empty. For all you could tell from his eyes, he could have been watching CNN.

Then he pushed the blade into his stomach about belt level and cut slowly across his entire belly, then started cutting up, then cut over again right under his ribs until he cut his aorta and all this blood went spurting out. And the whole time he's got this real serious, concentrated look. Concentrated but somehow empty. Like nothing could get to him.

I decided to skip the bath, get straight down to business. I sat on the floor in my room, took my T-shirt off and wrapped it around the blade of Mom's boning knife. I tried to put this real serious look on my face. Then I realized I had forgotten about the poem. The poem seemed more crucial than the bath, so I got up and took some paper out, sat down. But then my pen wouldn't work. I was starting to feel frustrated, like everything was falling apart.

Concentrate, I told myself. *Be the reflection of the moon on a still pond.*

I took a breath, got another pen, wrote a poem.

> *My enemies*
> *Can cheat me.*
> *But no one cheats*
> *Death.*

Which I thought was pretty cool.

Then I wrapped my shirt around the knife again and sat on the floor and tried to put the serious expression on my face again. I felt all sweaty and weird and tired.

I pushed the knife against my stomach. It kind of hurt, but didn't seem to be doing much. I pushed harder. It hurt like a bitch. But it still didn't stick into me at all.

I looked at the point of the knife. It was totally dull.

I was like, "Damn it!"

But secretly I was relieved.

On Monday I waited until Mom and Dad left for work, then went
down in the basement and got out my grandpa's old wheelchair.
He had stayed with us while he was dying of brain cancer, so there
was all this medical junk down in the basement. I found some
bandages and some tape. I wrapped the bandages around my
head so that my left eye was covered up and then put the wheelchair in the back of my car and drove to school. I waited in the
parking lot until pretty much everybody was inside the building,
then I got the wheelchair out real quick and sat in it and rolled it
into the front door of the school.

Mindy Edison was standing there outside the office. She stared
at me. "God!" she said. "What happened to you?"

"I chy to ki' mysel'," I said. I sort of let my tongue hang out
like Mr. Gilliland's did. Then I rolled past her into the office and
handed this sealed envelope to the secretary. The letter inside was
printed on stationery with my mom and dad's name at the top. I
knew what it said because I had typed it up myself.

```
Dear Dr. Oliphant:
Our son, Mark Hanson, Jr., a sophomore at
Hillandale, suffered a grievous wound on Sat-
urday. He attempted suicide with a gun. Because
of a mechanical failure in the weapon, he was
only injured and did not die. However, he has
lost all use of his legs; and his left eye prob-
```

ably will have to be surgically removed sometime
in the next week or two. He has also suffered a
slight cognitive deficit, which we are hoping is
only temporary.

Do not be alarmed. His physical condition is
stable. Dr. Rex Masterman, the chief surgeon at
Hillandale Hospital, tells us that his situation
will be best served if he returns to his "normal
routine" as quickly as possible.

We apologize for any inconvenience this may
cause and hope you will pray for his recovery.

Sincerely yours,

Mark and Rachel Hanson

I left the envelope on the counter and rolled to first period.
Ray and Eleanor watched me as I crept slowly into English class,
bumping into things like I couldn't really control my wheels.

"What happened, dude?" Ray said.

I turned my head really, really slowly and looked at him with
this really, really sad expression. Then I turned slowly back and
stared at the board, letting my tongue hang out. I amazed myself by not even halfway laughing. I started getting this sad feeling inside, almost like I actually *had* shot myself and scrambled
my brains.

By second period the word got around school that I had tried to
kill myself. Everybody got all quiet when I rolled by with the retard
expression on my face and my tongue hanging out. It was amazing

what a great act I did. Sometimes I even let a little drool come out, and pretty soon I had this round, wet stain on my T-shirt.

Everybody tried not to stare. But they couldn't help themselves.

After geometry class, Eleanor came up and stood in front of me with this strange expression on her face, staring at me like she was trying to figure something out. Finally she said, "I can't help what I did. I'm sorry. But I just got so sick of you lying all the time."

I just sort of looked at the floor. A long string of drool dripped off my tongue. She leaned over and wiped it off with the corner of her shirt. I could smell her Lady Speed Stick and for some reason it made me feel like crying.

Third period, we had an assembly. It was going to be one of these Say No to Drugs type deals—Officer Friendly and his drug-sniffing dog, all that crap.

Suddenly, as I rolled into the auditorium and saw the big banner with the red circle that said DRUGS in the middle with a big red slash through it, I had this idea. My heart started beating really hard.

I rolled my wheelchair up to the front of the auditorium, all the kids jumping out of my way like I was hitting them with a cattle prod. Dr. Oliphant, the principal, was up on the stage.

" 'Scuse me," I said. Kind of whispering as I looked up over the lip of the stage. "Dr. O'phant? Dr. O'phant? Sir?"

Dr. Oliphant finally heard me. He came over to the edge of the stage with this nervous look on his face.

"How you doing, Mark?" he said. Far as I knew, it was the first time he'd ever spoken to me. Hillandale's a pretty big school, and I doubted he even knew my name before today.

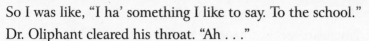

So I was like, "I ha' something I like to say. To the school."

Dr. Oliphant cleared his throat. "Ah . . ."

"This p'ogram? Iss about d'ugs, right? How bad d'ugs are?"

"Well . . ."

"After wha' happen to me—I ha' something to say to the schoo'. About why they shou'n't take d'ugs." I put this real sincere look on my face, still with my tongue hanging out. "Maybe I ca' help, make sure this ne'er happen to a'yone else." I was laying it on thick. I sort of lifted one hand, then let it flop down in my lap like it weighed about a ton.

He looked at me for a minute, then he said, "You're a very courageous young man."

So Officer Friendly got up there with the drug-sniffing dog and did his boring spiel, and everybody was shifting around in their chairs and snickering and stuff. Then when Officer Friendly wrapped up, Dr. Oliphant came to get me backstage and pushed my wheelchair out from behind the curtain.

Bang—total silence.

Everybody in the whole school was looking at me.

Dr. Oliphant rolled me across the stage and the wheels of Grandpa's wheelchair were squeaking on the floor. When he reached the microphone, he said, "Some of you may have heard what, ah, transpired to Mark Hanson this weekend. Well, we're talking about drugs today and all the terrible things they can do? I, uh . . ." Then he looked at me with this really sad expression and said to me, "Just speak from the heart, Mark."

He pushed the gooseneck microphone on the podium down to my level. It made this big *SSKRROONNNNKKKK* noise like some humongous robot ripping a giant electronic fart.

But nobody laughed. Total silence.

My heart was just banging away so fast it felt like it was about to pop out of my ribs. But I was still keeping the retard expression on my face, my head hanging over on my chest.

Then I went, "I juss wan' to say . . ."

I could hear the fans in the ceiling blowing air into the room. Someone coughed. I looked out at the auditorium. Everybody in the whole school was looking at me with wide eyes. I realized I'd been at Hillandale all these years and it was like nobody had ever looked at me before. Not *really*. I wasn't some big jock, some senior who'd gotten accepted to Harvard, some beauty queen. I was just some guy that nobody ever looked at or paid the slightest bit of attention to. I hadn't realized until that moment just how much I'd hated being a nobody.

"I juss wan' to say, don't feel sorry fo' me." I blinked, look-ing around, all retarded and everything. "You shou' feel sorry fo' yourselves, because . . ."

I let the words hang there for a while. Watching the kids watching me. Oh, man, they were all so sorry for me. They pitied me so much. But they were scared of me, too. Because I'd done something. I had totally, totally, totally *done* something. Some-thing that wasn't normal or regular or boring. And that scared the poop out of them.

I saw Mindy Edison out there, staring at me with these wide china blue eyes. I could see her chest moving up and down, like she was about to hyperventilate. She was just *hanging* on my words, dude. *Hanging!* I looked around some more. There was Ray: his skin was all white and clammy-looking. He glanced away as soon as he saw me looking at him.

". . . because . . ." I whispered into the microphone.

Then I spotted Eleanor. She wasn't sitting next to Ray. She was about five rows down, sitting by herself, arms crossed tight over her chest. Like maybe she'd had some kind of argument with Ray. Our eyes met. We stared at each other for a while. She was looking all weird and sad. And then suddenly, she kind of jerked and her face got hard. She must have seen it finally, read my bluff, seen something that told her this was all a big lie.

"Feel sorry for yourselves . . ." I said again. ". . . because . . ."

Then I stood up really fast, ripping the bandage off my head and chucking it into the audience the way rock stars throw their guitar picks out into the crowd. I yanked the microphone up to my lips—*SKKEEROOOOOOONNNNNNNGGGKK!!!!*

". . . because you're all suckers and losers and dumb-ass retards!"

Man, you should have been there. That's all I can say. You should have been there.

Next thing I know, Coach Peavey's got my arms and Mr. Rathrock has my feet and they're dragging me off and I'm still yelling and yelling and yelling.

"You're losers! You're suckers! You'd believe anything! I hate you! I hate you all!"

I got back from the loony bin last week.

Actually I kind of liked being there. It gave me a lot of time to read up on poker, learn the strategies, memorize the odds. Did you know the chances of being dealt a straight flush in five cards are one in sixty-four thousand, nine hundred and seventy-three?

But that's not the main thing in poker. Odds and strategies

and all that stuff? Nah, the main thing in poker is that you have to fool people into thinking they know you. When actually they don't.

See, my problem before was that people knew me. Now? Now, they don't know anything about me at all. I practiced in the mirror at the crazy house, staring at myself for hours and hours until I was able to erase every single emotion from my face, empty it out, moonlight reflecting on the surface of a still pond. After a while it felt like I was looking at somebody else's face, somebody hard and quick and dangerous. Somebody unpredictable. Somebody unknowable.

Anyway, I'm glad to be back in school now. After a while, being around crazy people gets on your nerves.

Funny thing, while I was away I turned into this sort of celebrity at Hillandale—the guy who wasn't afraid to do anything.

I talked to Mindy Edison at lunch today, told her a couple funny stories about wackos at the loony bin. I had my new face on, the face of a guy who's totally in charge, who can't be hurt or beaten or bamboozled. She kept looking at me with those wide blue eyes, and her beautiful chest moved quickly, like she was having trouble catching her breath, and I could see a vein throbbing wildly in her throat. Then she gave me her cell phone number. Without me even asking.

I played poker with Ray and Eleanor and the other guys last night. I took every last nickel they had. It was child's play.

I've got 'em fooled now. I've got 'em all fooled.

Walter Sorrells

Walter Sorrells is the author of The Hunted series. His most recent book is *The Silent Room*. Here's what he says about playing poker: "All modesty aside, in addition to being a ridiculously successful and famous writer, I'm generally recognized as being among the finest poker players in the history of the game. I began playing in high school, where my skills were so excellent that all my friends stopped playing with me. In eleventh grade I began playing professionally under the name Lefty Hillstomper. I have won the World Series of Poker six straight times. Plus I was a Navy SEAL, and a nationally ranked mixed martial arts fighter. And Angelina Jolie is my girlfriend."

Mr. Sorrells is also a big fat liar.

THE SCHOLARSHIP GAME

by Pete Hautman

"Hey Brainiac, what's seventy-two times nineteen?"

"My name is Tom," I say.

Adrian Canton opens his face into a fake look of surprise. "You don't know? C'mon, give us a number."

"Get lost, Adrian." Adrian is a senior scheduled to graduate next month. I can't imagine how.

I walk around him and his two oversize, underachieving cohorts. Rather, I *try* to walk around them. One of Adrian's meaty hands clamps onto my upper arm and shoves me against the wall of lockers. I am immobilized.

"Tell you what, *Tom*, answer the question. You get it right, I let you go. Get it wrong I kick your ass."

The answer, of course, is 1,368, but he won't know that. I say, "Seven hundred thirteen."

Adrian grins and releases me. "See?" he says to his friends. "The kid's a walking computer."

One of his moron friends is punching numbers into a calculator. Uh-oh.

I start walking away. The moron with the calculator looks up with a puzzled expression and says, "Hey!"

I take off down the hall running.

Only four weeks left till Adrian graduates.

Maybe I can avoid him until then.

It's not easy being a prodigy. I mean, the math part is easy. Want to know how far you've gone if the number of miles you've traveled equals half the number of inches of rope it takes to wrap 3,700 times around a 28-inch-diameter cylinder? I can tell you. The answer is 162,734, which happens to be the last six digits of my phone number.

Numbers are easy. Dealing with people, that's hard.

Especially when you're the only fourteen-year-old in the eleventh grade.

Unless you're playing a game. Games have rules, and rules are the great equalizer.

I'm good at games. I am an excellent chess player, for example, but my favorite game is poker. In fact, the guys I used to play with don't invite me anymore, because I usually win. I always remember which cards have been played, I know the odds, and I am very observant about the other players. Poker players have *tells*—unconscious things they do that can *tell* you what they've got—if you know what to look for.

I know what to look for.

After school I am waiting in line for my bus when I hear, "Hey Brainiac."

Uh-oh. Adrian Canton again.

I turn toward the voice, ready to run or get hit, but instead of Adrian and his moronic sidekicks, it's just Adrian, and he's wearing a friendly smile.

"You really got me this morning," he says. "Those guys will be kidding me till graduation."

I shrug. I can't bring myself to say I'm sorry.

"I suppose you get pretty sick of people asking you to do math tricks."

"It depends," I say, wondering what he wants from me.

"I mean, it would be like if guys kept coming up to me and asking me to lift a three-hundred-pound barbell over my head."

I look up at him, wondering whether he can actually lift that much.

Adrian says, "I just want you to know I don't have any hard feelings. I mean, it was really pretty funny." He laughs. I laugh too, only not as loud or as long.

He clears his throat and moves in closer. I tense up again.

"So, how'd you like to help me out with a little project?" he asks.

Now I'm really suspicious. When a guy like Adrian talks about a "little project" you know it's not building a birdhouse.

"Like what?" I say.

"Just let me borrow that brain of yours for a bit."

"My brain's pretty happy right where it is."

"I'm not gonna take it out. I just need some advice."

"What kind of advice?"

"Poker advice. Friday night I'm playing in the Scholarship Game."

Some say the Scholarship Game goes back to the 1950s, others say it is even older. Either way, it's been going on since before I was born. My dad remembers it from when he was in high school, and my grandfather claims to have played in it—and lost—back in 1968. According to local legend, the Game started when a group of high school seniors who could not afford college agreed to bet all their savings on a poker game. They played until all but one of them went broke, and the winner won enough to pay his first year's tuition. The Scholarship Game has been an annual event ever since.

"Fifteen hundred bucks to enter," Adrian says. "Winner take all."

"Wait a sec," I say. "*You* want to go to *college*?"

Adrian laughs. "Nobody uses Game money for college anymore. I want the money to start up a detailing shop. You know, fixing up cars. Look, I've got a seat in the game, and I just need, you know, a few tricks of the trade. I hear you're some kind of poker expert."

"You want me to teach you how to play poker? In *three days*?"

"I know how to *play*; I want you to teach me how to *win*."

I look back at the line of kids filing onto the bus. "My bus is loading."

"Forget the bus. I'll give you a ride home."

I have a bad feeling. I should hop on that bus and leave him to the mercy of his own clouded mind. Teach Adrian Canton how to play winning poker? It would be easier to teach a dog to talk.

"Look, Brainiac—"

"My name is Tom."

"Sorry. *Tom*. I just need a few tips is all. None of these other guys are any good; I played with them all before. I'm just trying to improve my odds."

Maybe Adrian is not a complete moron after all. He knows exactly how stupid he is, which is not quite so stupid that he doesn't know to ask for help.

"So what's in it for me?" I ask.

"A percentage of my winnings. If I win ten thousand, I'll give you a hundred bucks."

"That's only one percent."

"Okay, two hundred."

"That's only two percent."

"Yeah, but it's two hundred bucks."

"And if you don't win, I get nothing?"

"If I don't win, I'll be *broke*."

"Fifteen percent."

"*What?*"

"Fifteen percent. That's my price."

"You're crazy if you think I'm paying you that much for a couple of lessons."

"I'm not talking a couple of lessons here, Adrian. If you want to win this thing, I have to be right there, at the game, inside your head."

I hear the hiss of the door closing and I turn back just in time to see the bus pulling away from the curb.

"How would you do that?" Adrian asks.

Drover's Lodge is the sort of seedy motel that caters to people who can't afford a Motel 6. There may even be some drovers there, whatever a drover is, but I don't see any. I haul my bike up to the second floor walkway and lock it to the railing, then knock on the door to room 230. A few seconds later the door is opened by a red-faced beanpole with longish hair, a Chicago Cubs baseball cap and sunglasses. It takes me a second to recognize him as Towering Tad Feider, a semi-disreputable senior who would probably have been kicked out of school if he wasn't the top scorer on the basketball team. A cloud of cigarette smoke and laughter filters past him.

"Hey Tad," I say.

"Brainiac?" he says, peering down at me. "What are you doing here?"

"I came to watch," I say.

"Sorry, kid. Private game."

"I'm with Adrian," I say.

"Is that Brainiac?" I hear Adrian shout. "Let him in!"

Tad scowls, shrugs, then stands aside to let me in.

"He's my protégé," Adrian says. "I told the kid I'd show him some moves."

It's all I can do to not laugh.

Like tennis, chess, or boxing, poker is a game of skill. It is also a game of luck. But in the long run, skill trumps luck. The best player gets the money in the end.

I look over the crew surrounding the round, felt-covered table.

Towering Tad Feider is all but guaranteed to lose. The reason he is top scorer on the basketball team is because he takes every conceivable shot, and makes a fair percentage of them. He'll probably try to bluff every other hand.

To Tad's left, Joe Hutchinson (better known as Hutch) is hunched over his pile of chips looking as nervous as a small dog guarding a big bowl. Hutch will be scared to bet his good hands, and easy to bluff. Jimmy Wilson and Tyler Crossman are smoking cigarettes and drinking beer. Drunks practically give their money away at the poker table. Sitting beside Tyler is Perry Gelfman, a meek, friendly sort who just wants people to like him. He doesn't have that killer instinct.

The last player is Jamie Wagner, a toadlike kid with taped-up glasses, oily hair, and fuzzy teeth. Jamie is a fellow member of the chess club. I beat him the last three times we played. Jamie does not like losing, and he does not much care for me. I wonder how he got the money to buy into the game. Everybody knows that the Wagners are poor as dirt.

Seven players.

Adrian pulls out a wad of cash, counts out $1,500, and hands it to Tad.

"Plus five for the pizza," Tad says.

Seven times $1,500 is $10,500.

Adrian hands over his last five dollars. Tad puts the money in a cigar box and gives Adrian a rack of chips.

Fifteen percent of $10,500 is $1,575.

I take my place standing behind Adrian, already thinking about how I'm going to spend my share.

The game is five card stud. By tradition, the Scholarship Game has always been five stud: one card down and four cards up, with a bet after each up card. The ante is five dollars, and all betting is no limit.

For the first hour, I hardly play a hand. Or rather, Adrian hardly plays a hand. We've worked out a code. I touch his right arm, he knows to bet or raise. I touch his left arm, it tells him to call. I do nothing, he knows to check, or fold if there is a bet. Mostly I've been standing behind him doing nothing. I'm not going to throw away our money on mediocre cards. And I need time to watch the other players for tells.

Ty Crossman, for instance, gets very quiet when he has a good hand. When he has a great hand, his face goes rigid. That's a tell. Hutch Green is the opposite. When he likes his cards he becomes animated, sitting forward and talking more than usual. That's another tell. Tad has a pretty good poker face, but he likes to bluff too much, and I notice that when he's bluffing he pushes his chips out without counting them. But when Tad counts out his chips, look out! Perry Gelfman, on the other hand, doesn't bluff at all. He goes into every hand expecting to lose, and he usually does.

Jamie Wagner is tougher to read. He has a face like a rubber mask.

I watch and I wait.

Adrian is getting frustrated. He wants to get in there and gamble, but I'm making him fold hand after hand.

Then Adrian gets a pair of tens in his first two cards. He wants to bet so bad he can taste it, but Ty Crossman has a king showing, and his face has gone blank as a Roman statue, so when Ty bets fifty dollars, I do nothing. Adrian turns and glares at me. I stare back at him until he shrugs and pitches his hand into the discard pile.

It turns out that Ty has a pair of kings, as I suspected. He wins $200 from Tad, who was betting on a smaller pair.

After that, Adrian doesn't give me any more dirty looks.

Hutch Green is the first player to go broke when his aces and tens lose to Tad Feider's jack-high straight.

Paying the five-dollar ante each hand slowly erodes Adrian's bankroll. He's getting nervous. Everybody in the room is jittery. None of them have ever played for this kind of money before. Two hours into the game, Tad Feider has the biggest stack with $2,400. Jamie Wagner has a little over $1,900. The rest of us are roughly even with around $1,000 each, give or take. But this is no-limit poker. One big hand can change everything. One mistake, and it's all over.

Adrian picks up another pair of tens. Ty, whose upcard is an ace, bets fifty dollars, his usual opening bet. Adrian is about to throw away his cards when I let my hand brush his left elbow, telling him to call. I feel him tense up. He is confused. The last time he had tens, I told him to throw them away. But this time I'm reading Ty as weak.

Everybody else folds. On the next card Ty gets a nine, Adrian a king. Ty bets out again, this time shoving $300 into the pot.

I raise my hand to stifle a cough, touching Adrian's right shoulder on the way. Adrian goes rigid. The touch high on his shoulder tells him to raise the size of the pot, $430, almost half of our remaining chips. Adrian hesitates, then shoves his money in. Ty makes a sour face, looks at his hole card, rolls his eyes and throws his hand away.

I smile. I knew he was bluffing.

Shortly thereafter, Tad loses all his money to Jamie in an insane suicide bluff with a queen-high. It's almost as though he loses it deliberately.

I start to wonder about Tad and Jamie.

Ty and Jimmy last longer, but eventually get knocked out. By midnight it's down to Adrian, Perry, and Jamie. Perry is down to the felt, fingering his last few chips nervously. Jamie and Adrian are about even. Perry has been playing cautiously but predictably—Adrian and I have been picking up pot after pot by betting into him when he shows weakness. But it's Jamie the toad who finishes Perry off with two pair, queens and jacks.

It's down to two players. At this point, luck becomes a huge factor. The secret is to rely on luck as little as possible. I have been studying Jamie for hours. He's a rock, a stone, a closed book. He plays tight as knot, and it is almost impossible to read him.

Notice I say "almost."

When Jamie has good cards he keeps one hand close to them, as if he's afraid someone is going to snatch them away. When his cards are not so good, he plays with his chips, picks his nose, scratches his chin, or whatever. I am able to escape a few nasty beats by folding early when I see his hand hovering near his cards.

By midnight, we are dead even, with $5,250 each.

We go back and forth, betting and folding, folding and betting, pushing the antes back and forth with neither of us gaining an advantage. Hutch is dealing for us now—we agreed that whoever won would pay him a hundred dollars. Tad is standing behind Jamie, drinking beer and watching us play. Everybody else has left.

"You guys play like little old ladies," Tad says.

Adrian does not like this comment. He is tired, he's impatient, and he has no respect for Jamie's play. To him, Jamie is a nerd, beneath contempt. The next hand, Jamie bets $250 on a king. Adrian, without instructions from me, raises to $1,000 with a jack, ten. Jamie immediately shoves in four stacks of chips, about $3,000.

"Go get 'em, kid," Tad says to Jamie. "Let's wrap this up and go home."

Jamie's hand is near his cards. He has something. Inside, I am screaming at Adrian: *Fold! Fold, you fool!*

Adrian stares glumly at Jamie's raise. His hands play with his chips, stacking and restacking . . . an eternity later, Adrian sighs and throws away his cards. I turn and walk out the door. I am unlocking my bike from the railing when Adrian comes after me.

"What are you doing?" he asks.

"I'm leaving."

"Why? We got him on the run."

"Look," I say, keeping my voice low, "we had an agreement. You play the way I tell you to play. You were supposed to fold that crappy hand. Why the hell did you raise?"

"I was pretty sure he was bluffing."

"Bluffing? He had you beat with the king!"

"Okay, I made a mistake. One little hand."

"Little? Five minutes ago we were even. Now he's got us out-chipped by more than a grand. He can break us in one hand, while we need at least two big hands to bust him. You call that even?"

Adrian's shoulders drop as if the air has gone out of him. "You don't think we can win?"

"Not if you make another bonehead play."

"Okay, okay. I screwed up."

"There's something else you should know. I think Jamie is fronting for Tad."

"What do you mean?"

"You notice how interested Tad is in Jamie's cards? I think Tad bankrolled Jamie, then deliberately lost all his chips to him early on to give Jamie an advantage."

Adrian scowls, the shakes his head hard, like a wet dog drying itself. "Come on back inside," he says. "Let's finish him off."

Back and forth, betting and folding, folding and betting. Whoever has the high card showing bets, whoever has the low card folds. Jamie has $5,500 to our $5,000. I'm not about to take any chances. We go back and forth for an hour, and then for another hour, with neither of us pulling ahead.

Jamie keeps giving me this flat, toadlike stare. I think he's figured out that Adrian is my puppet, but at this point I don't care. He and Tad are just as guilty.

Shortly after 1:00 A.M. Adrian picks up a pair of black kings. Jamie has the jack of spades showing. His hand is near his cards, meaning he likes them, but the best thing he could have would be a pair of jacks. I do nothing, telling Adrian to check.

I'm setting a trap.

Jamie bets $1,000. I bump Adrian's left elbow with my hip, and he calls the bet.

Our next card is a queen of hearts. Jamie gets the ten of spades. I have Adrian check again, hoping to get another bet out of Jamie. Jamie thinks for a few seconds, looks at me, and checks behind us. I'm disappointed; I was hoping to check-raise him.

Hutch deals us our fourth card: a third king for Adrian and the nine of spades for Jamie.

I cough, my signal to Adrian that I need time to think.

We have three kings, the best possible hand at the moment. But there is one card yet to come, and Jamie has the ten, jack, and nine of spades showing. He could be drawing to a flush or a straight. Either hand would beat us. It is even possible that he has the queen, eight, or seven of spades in the hole, giving him a draw to a straight flush.

If Jamie has any spade, there are eight remaining cards that could give him a flush—Adrian already has the king of spades locked up. If Jamie has a straight draw, his odds are even worse. Worst case scenario, he's got about one chance in three of beating us.

Still, there's a lot of money at stake. Better to buy the pot right then and there, I decide, and not give Jamie a chance to draw a fifth card. I let my right hand fall to the top Adrian's shoulder. He pushes all of our chips into the pot.

"All-in," he says.

Jamie sits back in his chair and stares at our bet, at our two kings showing, at his own hand, and at me. I actually feel sorry for him. He *can't* call. He knows he's beat by the pair of kings we have showing.

Seconds pass.

"The bet's on you," Hutch tells him.

"I know, I know," says Jamie, chewing on his thumbnail now.

I am surprised that he's taking so long. There's really nothing else he can do but fold. The odds are against him, and he knows it. It would be insane. No one in their right mind would bet it all on a one-in-three draw—especially not a guy like Jamie.

So why is he taking so long?

I feel his unblinking amphibian stare on me, and suddenly I see something I overlooked: Jamie is *tired*. The whites of his eyes are red, the flesh beneath them is dark and saggy, and the rest of his pimply face is pale and bloodless. We've been playing for six hours. He's exhausted.

I see something else as well. I see hatred. He knows I've been calling the shots. He knows I've been outplaying him. And now I'm about to beat him out of $1,000 with my kings, shifting the balance of power to our side.

Of course, he wants to see that final card. Who wouldn't? But he can't. The numbers won't let him. In this game, numbers rule. I know it. Jamie knows it. He has no choice but to fold. I allow myself a little smile.

Jamie blinks his toady eyes at my smile.

Behind him, Tad towers as tense and rigid as a telephone pole.

Suddenly, as if a dam has broken inside him. Jamie's hands come up and he shoves his chips into the pot.

"Call," he says. He smiles, showing me his fuzzy, greenish teeth.

My stomach turns into a lead balloon. There is a timeless interlude when nothing moves, there is no actual sound, nothing but a stretched-out moment when I hear Jamie's voice inside my head, and I am sure he is saying, *Screw you, Brainiac.*

I misjudged him. I didn't add in all the factors.

I didn't add in that he is tired.

I didn't calculate his hatred for me.

And I forgot to include the biggest factor of all: Jamie is playing for Tad. It's *not his money.*

He is grinning openly now, the grin of a madman who has stepped into an abyss, as he flips up his hole card. Black Mariah. Queen of spades.

I swallow and will my heart to slow. What am I worried about? The odds are still in our favor. It's gonna be okay.

Adrian turns up our hole card, revealing the king of spades. Jamie's mouth tightens, then he shrugs. The king hurts him, but not that much. He already knew he needed a flush or a straight to beat us.

Hutch deals Adrian his fifth and final card.

I can't believe what I see. The case cowboy—the last king in the deck! Four freaking beautiful lovely amazing unbelievable kings!

I hear Adrian suck his breath in. Jamie's eyes grow muddier

and his lids slide down to cover them halfway. He's toast, and he knows it. Behind him, Tad groans.

Only one card in the deck can help him now. He needs a straight flush to beat our four cowboys, and only the eight of spades will give it to him.

The numbers are good. Our odds could hardly be better. Adrian turns and gives me a high five.

Maybe I can't always count on human behavior, but numbers are solid. Numbers are real. There is only one eight of spades in the deck—one card out of 43 remaining in the deck can give him a straight flush. One card.

"Here it comes," whispers Tad in a hoarse voice.

Slowly, milking the moment for maximum drama, Hutch turns up Jamie's final card.

I am walking down the hallway at school juggling an armload of books when somebody slaps me, hard, on the back of the head. I fly forward onto my belly, skidding across the hard linoleum on a tide of books.

"Hey, Brainiac, you dropped your books."

I look up at Adrian Canton. The expression on his face is neither angry nor amused. He actually looks a little sad.

I start picking up my books. He watches until I've gathered them all, then knocks them out of my arms.

"Dropped 'em again, Brainiac," he says.

Three more weeks until Adrian graduates.

I look up at his bland face.

It's going to be a long three weeks.

Pete Hautman

Pete Hautman's books have won numerous awards, including the 2004 National Book Award for his novel *Godless*. His most recent novels include *Rash*, a young adult novel set in the year 2074, and *The Prop*, a poker-themed crime novel.

Pete has been playing poker since he was eight years old. He lives with novelist and poet Mary Logue in Minnesota and Wisconsin. Hautman and Logue are currently collaborating on *The Bloodwater Mysteries*, a mystery series for middle-grade readers. The first two books in the series are *Snatched* and *Skullduggery*.

UP THE RIVER

by Will Weaver

It was important to lose once in a while. The online poker security geeks needed to see that Riverboy24 was only human. That would be Seth Parker, sixteen-year-old, blond-haired, blue-eyed "Mr. Everything" at LaCrosse High School. A few grand in the hole was no big deal because, with his new system, he could win it back anytime he wanted.

Tonight he was getting low on chips,

but building himself a table image. IdahoSpud was scared of him, but the more aggressive HotchaGotcha kept calling him down, forcing Riverboy to show his hand. Like the time Riverboy raised on the river with nothing but a king high, and HotchaGotcha called him with pocket deuces.

Just like that—ka-zing—he was down 300 bucks and now close to three grand of real money on his Visa and MasterCard. Enough success for one night. He logged off and went downstairs for a 2 A.M. glass of milk and some cookies.

"Calc done?" his mother murmured sleepily from the couch. She was a night owl like him, and in the dark living room was reading by the light of a small lamp; the TV whispered across from her. She never seemed to watch it, but liked having it on while she read. His father was an early-to-bed guy.

"In the bag," he answered. Calculus was his excuse for staying up all hours, but there was a lot of math in poker—statistics, actually—if one were serious about the game, and so it was not a total lie. He bent over and kissed the top of her head—and in the lamp's light saw a distinct line of pure white roots below her auburn hair. He drew back. His mother colored her hair? How come he never knew that?

"Thanks, dear," she said, patting his arm; her eyes stayed on her book.

He headed to the kitchen.

"Anything going on at school tomorrow?" she asked in her parent-on-automatic-pilot voice.

"Champagne brunch after history class, then meth lab all afternoon."

"Good, dear," she murmured. "Have your snack, then get to bed."

As he passed by the television, a tidy, handsome guy stood before a chart. Some infomercial. Make Big Money By Working At Home! You, Too, Can Supplement Your Income by $500, even $1,000 A Month, the chart read. "I know, because I did," the man said. "Call now. Operators are standing by."

"What, dear?" his mother asked.

"Nothing."

"You laughed."

"Did I? Must be the calc. It always feels so good to be done."

"That's nice, dear," she said.

Seth soon thumped up the stairs two at a time. His life was all good. There ought to be a law against a life like his. Parents who left him alone. Sweet SAT scores. Junior class president. College apps in with a lock on Madison, and Stanford not out of reach. Captain of the golf team. Plus his "night job" making money the fun way, playing poker; if his parents only knew how easy it was.

Online poker, thanks to Riverboy and his very special friend, Musclebound690, was like a license to print money. In his darkened bedroom the two buddies sat side by side pulsing their wallpaper, ready for action. Riverboy's screen had a quiet stream flowing through a meadow; Musclebound had a big Dodge truck overflowing with bikini-clad bimbos (it was important, online, to have two distinct personas). "Sorry, boys—no more action tonight," he said sternly. "You two are spending too much time together. People will talk."

He lay in bed but couldn't sleep. Something about his mother's white hair freaked him out—not so much that her hair was turning gray but that he should have known that she colored it. That it had sneaked up and blindsided him. He prided himself on avoiding surprises.

To clear his head he got up and let Musclebound out for some exercise. A few hands on Pokerhead.com. It was important that Musclebound and Riverboy play alone on occasion; that they not always be online simultaneously. As a player Musclebound was a crapshooter who took crazy chances on occasion. Tonight, for example, Musclebound was playing no-limit and decided to go all-in four hands in a row with garbage cards. It worked the first three times, but then he got called by a guy named Clancy, who had an ace-king. That one had cost Musclebound two hundred bucks.

Seth reloaded and won most of it back, ending up with a reasonable loss of forty bucks, a good night for a meathead like Musclebound, then logged off. Yes he was down $2,800, but had been up as high as $6,000. Bankrolling was all about long-term strategy. His goal was $10,000, at which point he would cash out and wait ten days for the check in the mail. Or not cash out; maybe he'd shoot for twenty grand. A car, college money—it was all possible as long as he stayed on plan. Which included a losing streak once in a while.

At school the next morning, Shane Jackson, a senior wrestler, blocked his path. Seth braced himself for pain of some kind. But Shane, his breath rank from Mountain Dew and chew, said, "Hey Golden Boy, wanna play some poker tonight?"

"Me?" Seth said.

"Yeah you, numb-nuts. I hear you're pretty good."

"I get lucky once in a while," Seth replied in his best male double entendre if-you-know-what-I-mean voice. He could muster that shit when he had to.

"Me too. You should check out that new, short blonde chick, Sara, from tenth grade."

"Thanks for the tip," Seth said gamely.

"Anyway, a few of us boys are meeting in the equipment room after practice. Coaches are gone, we're going to play a little holdem. Be there, okay?"

"Ummm. Maybe. I'll see. I'll try."

"Try hard. I'm expecting you," Shane said and rocked Seth's chest with a "friendly" fist-thump.

Seth coughed, rubbed the sore spot on his chest, and made his way through the crowd to his locker. As a rule, he did not play poker with idiots and fools. There were plenty of those games to be had with LaCrosse high schoolers, or drunken college kids in the dorms at the nearby state college. They were easy marks but the stakes were too low, plus he couldn't take the conversation. "That new girl, the red-haired skank, Jade? I bet she's easy."

Or: "Chevies are squat. You want a real truck, get a Ford 250."

Or: "I had the dry heaves for twenty-four hours—I'm not kidding."

Why did guys who played poker think swearing, spit cups for their chew plus backward caps and sunglasses were written into the rules of Texas holdem? College guys were worse, with their pizza farts and incessant remarks about chicks they had scored with, chicks who were a "sure thing" (so why were they all jammed into a methane-filled dorm room playing cards with other boys?). On the other hand, a few hands of live poker with knuckleheads couldn't hurt—in fact, it might keep him sharp for his real game. Which was online poker.

He had always liked cards and was always online, so why not poker online? He started last winter, but took it slowly. Did his research. Began as a silent railbird, then got his sea legs in play-money games. Within a couple of weeks he got used to the "shkkk-shkkk" of the electronic shuffle; the tiny digital chips zipping across the little green table; the cartoon-like, seated characters calling, betting and folding without moving a digital muscle. It was like real poker but without the cigarette smoke, without the lame conversation and the farts. Don't like a player's chat? Drop the cursor on his head and mute him. Online poker was a tidy, faster, more efficient game.

After he got comfortable with the online poker game he took a deep breath late one night and threw down his "Junior" MasterCard. Made a deposit on Pokerhead.com. His card had a $500 credit line ("For emergencies only," his parents had said); he bought fifty bucks worth of real-money chips, receiving ten dollars of "bonus chips." His first real-money action was in a 25/50 cent low-stake limit game with a maximum bet of fifty cents; after two hours, he was up ten bucks. Delivering pizzas paid better, but this was fun.

Once he found that there were the same idiots and fools online as there were in real life, he moved ahead into $1/$2 games. Then $3/$6, which brought his hourly "pay" (he kept track) to over ten dollars an hour. Any time he wanted it. Moving to $5/$10 games felt like a big jump, but he was a by-the-numbers player who folded six or seven times out of ten, and he stayed in the black—and then some. So it felt perfectly natural for him to start playing no-limit. At the end of his first full month he had a bank-roll of more than 300 bucks; by the end of three months, he was $1,500 to the good.

His reality check came very late one night when he caught pocket aces in a no-limit game and raised twenty bucks. HosA-CanUC, holding a piece-of-crap K-J (he would learn later), called. The flop was 3-Q-10. Seth bet a hundred bucks—best to take the pot down right away, he figured. HosA with his Kojak now had four cards to a straight (K-Q-J-10). HosA thought for a few seconds, the timer on the screen ticking down, then raised all-in for $1,387—enough to put Seth all-in.

Seth called; after all, he had bullets, he was flying with American Airlines—AA—(which should have been his first clue: all the airlines were going bankrupt).

Since there could be no more betting, both hands were re-vealed. Seth still liked his hand. HosA was a big dog to win—he needed a nine or an ace to make his straight, or two running kings, or two running jacks for three-of-a-kind (a king and a jack wouldn't help him, because that would give Seth a straight). But on the river, HosA caught a nine and beat Seth's pocket rockets with a straight. All in all, a horrible bad beat—his pocket aces cracked by some donkey playing a king-jack off-suit.

Just like that his bankroll disappeared. Pissed off, flushed and sweaty, he bought another $300 on credit and lost again. After two more hands, it was clear he was on tilt. Getting a grip, he pulled the plug and went to bed. Lay there waiting for his heart-beat to slow. Suddenly he had close to $500 racked up on his credit card.

Not that his parents monitored his credit card. After all, he was junior class prez and good at math and went to church and visited his granny and was able to handle his own affairs. But it was the principle of the thing. He was not in this to lose money, certainly not to some dumb-shit lucky lone ranger out there. Bottom line: He wanted his money back. Plus it wasn't like his family was rich. His parents didn't know anything about money, which is why they never really had any, and now he was following suit. Which only made him more angry. A little shame, a little rage was the mother of invention, and it suddenly came to him: Why not help himself out?

He had heard about online cheating. Two friends sharing hole cards on the phone or through instant messaging, *collusion* was the technical term. The idiot players at high school all talked about how easy it was to make money by cheating at online poker. Like anything—like math—it was a matter of problem-solving in clear, logical steps.

Two computers, two Internet connections, two credit cards, two separate addresses. That was his epiphany. It was easy for the online goons to trace multiple accounts to the same computer, the same Internet provider address. But what if everything was totally separate? How were they to know?

This took some thought and a few minor fibs—okay, a couple of lies—to get set up, but his parents (father an English professor, mother a musician) were easy to work around. He was the "baby" of three kids, had never caused them any trouble; right now they were full-blown middle-aged clichés, always on-the-go, the kind of parents you see on television commercials, caught up in trying to stay "active." "Yes, dear," they could see the need for a new laptop "for school" and the logic of keeping the old one for data backup. The Swansons, bone-head next-door neighbor family, had unencrypted home wireless humming fifty feet outside his bedroom window, which solved his need for a second IP address. And his dear old gran, Sarah Perkins (S. Perkins) lived in Havenwood, an assisted living joint on the other side of town, which solved that pesky issue of the separate street address for his other credit card. Technically the Visa was in her name, a new account, but he was scrupulous about not using that one—at least not very often.

After school, he made his way down the worn, white granite steps, descending into the lower ring of gymnasium hell. He followed his nose to the locker room—one of his least favorite places. Not that he didn't dig athletics; he was just not a grabbing, tackling kind of male athlete. Guys with excessive testosterone annoyed him, and here they were, gathered in the rank-smelling football equipment room. Shane, Darren, Jaiden, Lance, Trevor, Sam—all wrestlers—plus several hangers-on. Musclebound himself, if he had a real body, would fit in well here.

"Thought you got lost, golf-boy," Shane said, glancing up briefly from his cards. A few dollar bills lay on the table along with small scatters of chips.

I just followed the smell. "Sorry, guys. Had to count my balls after practice."

There was appreciative grunting around the table.

"Darren's lost his for sure," Shane said. "All-in, dude."

"She-it," Darren drawled, and folded.

Seth wedged himself in between Jaiden and Lance. They were playing no-limit holdem. He bought five dollars' worth of chips and waited for the next hand.

His first two hole cards were seven-deuce—the worst possible starting cards; he laughed. The other players sat silent and stony-faced. Trevor wore sunglasses and cap pulled low, Sam wore wrap around, mirrored glasses. Clearly they'd been watching too many poker tournaments on television.

"Something funny?" Shane said.

"My cards," Seth replied.

"Funny ha-ha or funny bye-bye."

"We'll see, won't we?" Seth said.

He decided to make it interesting by betting his entire five bucks before the flop.

"Dude!" Shane said. "Slow down!"

"Got to bet my monster," Seth said.

Everybody folded, and Seth showed them the crap cards he'd bet on.

Now they were sure to call him down every time he bet. What he should have done was sit back and wait for some really good cards, but winning was not what he wanted. If he won, these guys would take it out on him in some other way, possibly involving blood and fractured bones. So Seth kept right on playing like an idiot, making sure to lose it all toward the end.

"I heard you were way better than that," Shane said, raking in the scattering of chips.

"Bad night. Everybody has them," Seth said, and shrugged.

"Bring more money next time," Shane said.

There was laughter at Seth's expense—all good in his mind—and finally, blessedly, he escaped up the stairs to sunlight and fresh air. As much as he hated live poker with jocks, he could always come back to this game and pay off his debts.

That night he excused himself early from the dinner table. "I've got a long night of it," he said, mustering a pained expression.

"Math?" his father said. "Not like I could help." He was a balding, middle-sized man with wire-rimmed glasses, a man who would have been first to die in the Donner Party. A cruel thought, yes, but Seth had always felt distant from his dad; he was a man with no edge, no discernable dark side, no capacity for risk—and certainly no way to ever make any more money than his teacher's salary.

"Yes, lots of calc," Seth said. He could feel Riverboy and Musclebound, upstairs, poised like runners at the blocks, waiting for action. "Gotta go."

He locked his door, cracked his knuckles and positioned himself between his two boys. Took a mouse in each hand.

First he logged in Riverboy. Waited a tasteful minute or two before signing in Musclebound. His combined credit card debt, MasterCard and Visa, was $2,800, but tonight was comeback time. No rush, just a nice steady grind for the next couple of weeks. According to his personal spreadsheet, by month's end he should be up six or seven thousand.

With Riverboy seated at the table, Musclebound took the most distant chair—which is when his computers froze. Not just one IP, but both. He swore, then looked over his shoulder at his door. No response from his parents.

Then his cursors came back but the games didn't. His screen filled with large font text underneath:

Pokerhead.com requests a photocopy of a government-issued ID or its equivalent, in order to verify the Player's identification. Player is tem-

porarily suspended and account frozen until ID verification is completed. We look forward to your continued business. Sincerely, Pokerhead.com.

This same message for both Riverboy and Musclebound. Plus directions on where to send the photocopies.

Seth swallowed. His hands went clammy. He leaned back from the screens. He logged off, waited a minute, then tried to log on again. Same message.

Downstairs, his parents looked up, surprised to see him. "I thought I'd take a break and drive over and see Gran," he said. "Haven't seen her in a while."

"She'd love that," his mom said. "You're so nice to her." She tousled his blond hair.

"I agree," his father said, and tossed him the car keys. "All work and no play—you know the rest of it, son."

"Sure. Thanks. Great," Seth said distractedly, and headed out.

Havenwood had three wings outside, and an overly clean smell inside. Like exploded air fresheners. Air fresheners gone wild. What smells they were covering up, he didn't want to know.

"Hey—it's my Buddy!" his gran exclaimed. She looked up from some kind of needlework.

"Hi, Gran." He bent to hug her, careful not to squeeze too hard; she was a slim woman whose very brown hair was done up in tight curls. Her pale skull showed through the thin curls.

"You usually come on the fifteenth of the month," she said.

"Really?" Seth answered. His hands went clammy again; was it that obvious?

"Yes. I keep track," she said, turning to her wall calendar, touching its tiny notes with a finger. The skin of her hand was papery thin; he could see every vein, tiny and blue, and the five cords, like little wires, to her fingers. Her eyes, however, were bright and lively. "One has to have something to do besides these ridiculous projects they give us," she said, turning back to him.

Seth helped her set the knitting aside. "Anything you need, Gran? Any mail that needs looking after?" he said.

She frowned. "Yes. You can sort through some of those credit card letters. I get more and more of these offers and 'free checks.' I worry that somebody will steal them."

"No problem, Gran. I'll take them home and get rid of them."

"Plus I've been getting these calls lately."

"Calls?" Seth said as he surreptitiously scanned the mail.

"Just today, someone asking me about poker."

"Poker?" Seth replied. The word came our thin and raspy, like from an old man's voice, but Gran didn't notice.

"Yes. Do I play poker, they asked. I couldn't understand what they were saying. They asked me all these questions, and finally I just had to hang up on him. They've called twice now."

The room shrank. Walls lurched closer. He smelled the smell behind the disinfectant, but it was not the odor of old people: It was his armpits.

"Poker? That's strange." He manufactured a short laugh. "Probably some telemarketer of some kind. It's best to not say anything to them—just hang up."

"You're probably right," she murmured, her pale forehead creased with worry.

"Really, Gran. Don't think a thing about those calls or the credit card stuff. I'll take care of everything."

A smile broke across her face like the sun coming up; something inside Seth shriveled up.

But not all the way.

After all, he thought as he left Havenwood, it was not like he was actually stealing from his own grandmother. He was just borrowing. Borrowing her address. Borrowing her driver's license, which he had sneaked from her bedside drawer before he left. It was not like she was going to drive anywhere.

On the way back home he stopped at a copy shop and photocopied her license, then his. According to Pokerhead.com instructions, he signed her name (he knew her crampy little signature) on one affidavit, then his name on the other. Then, in separate envelopes, and after driving across town to different post office branches, he mailed them to Pokerhead's business office.

When he got home, his parents were pleased to see him and asked him the usual questions about Gran—when the phone rang. Neither parent made a move to answer it.

"I'm sure it's for you," his mother said. "Something about poker? I had no idea what they wanted. Told them to call back when you'd be home."

The phone rang again, louder than he had ever heard it. Seth made no move to answer it. "Must have the wrong house," he said with a shrug. "Or its some clever telemarketer. Don't answer it; they'll go away," he said.

"Is that Gran's mail?" his mother asked.

"Just some credit card stuff I told her I'd shred. She worries about everything."

"One has to be cautious," his father said. "There's that whole identity-theft thing one reads about."

No one could steal your identity, Dad, because you don't have one. "I suppose you're right; I'll get rid of these right now." With that, Seth escaped to his room.

Just in case this was all a mistake, he tried to log on to Pokerhead. But the same message—Identify Confirmation Alert—came up. He turned to Gran's mail. Several new credit card applications, but pay dirt in the pile. Zero percent interest checks from Visa: Use these checks to take advantage of Super Low Rates! Write a check to yourself, make home improvements, go on a well-deserved vacation. First check zero percent interest (fixed APR for limited duration), the second and third check only 4.99 percent until balance is paid in full.

To cover his Visa card balance, he wrote a check from Gran's card; it was, after all, only temporary until he could get back online.

He did not sleep well the next three nights. Felt edgy from not playing. He found a couple of games after school and won twenty bucks, but it was not the same rush as playing online. Several times a night he tried Pokerhead.com, but the same message came up; he was sure they had received the photo IDs by now.

Then, eureka, a new message from Pokerhead:

Please resume play. We look forward to your continued business.

"Wake up, boys, we're back in the saddle!" he said—then lowered his voice. He busted a brief wild jig about the room, cleared his desk of schoolwork, and got down to business. He logged both computers on, found empty seats at a no-limit table with blind bets of $2 and $4, and got down to business.

Online collusion is almost as much of an art as poker itself. The trick is to wait for a big hand, then whipsaw some poor sucker into putting way more money into the pot than he normally would.

It takes patience, waiting for just the right situation to appear.

That night, Seth and his two colluding avatars played for an hour before finding an opportunity. Musclebound had a three-eight—a garbage hand. Riverboy had pocket kings. Riverboy called the $4 blind, a guy named Finkster called behind him, and Musclebound put in the minimum raise. The idea was to build the pot a little before the flop, give Finkster something substantial to lust after.

Both Finkster and Riverboy just called Musclebound's raise.

The flop came ace-king-trey. Ka-ching! Trip kings—this was perfect! Seth crossed his fingers, hoping that Finkster had an ace in his hand. If he did, his pair of aces would cost him plenty.

Riverboy checked.

Finkster made a bet about the size of the pot. Musclebound, with his worthless three-eight, smooth-called.

Riverboy raised it twenty-five dollars, just a little raise—not so much as to scare Finkster out of the pot. Finkster called.

Musclebound raised another twenty-five.

Riverboy raised twenty-five more.

It would cost Finkster $50 to call, but there was more than $200 in the pot now. He wouldn't be able to resist.

Finkster called.

Time to set the hook.

Musclebound raised another $50. Riverboy raised all-in.

Finkster thought for almost his entire allotted thirty seconds, then called with his last $187.

Musclebound folded. Seth did not want Musclebound to have to show down his three-eight—if Finkster knew that Musclebound had been betting with nothing he'd have known he was being cheated.

Because they were both all-in, Riverboy's and Finkster's cards were turned face up. Finkster had an ace-king. He was drawing dead—no way for him to win. Seth gave himself a high five . . . which is when his computer screens went stiff. Froze like a winter lake in Superior. Same message, both screens:

Security and integrity of Pokerhead.com is foremost. Computer monitoring tracks IP addresses, surveys suspicious betting, automatically calls up all hand histories and cross-references with all other online gaming sites. Violations herewith suggest collusion between Riverboy24 (Seth Parker, Lacrosse, Wisconsin) and Musclebound690 (Sarah Parker, Lacrosse, Wisconsin). Both accounts are hereby closed; all assets/ bonus chips declared null and void; all addresses banned from this and participating online poker sites. Have a nice day.

Much later, he went downstairs for a snack. His mother was reading by her small lamp, and as usual he went over—forced himself—and gave her a quick kiss on the hair. But she sensed something—something in his silence, his walk—and looked up.

"Is everything all right, honey?"

"Sure."

"You look pale. Really tired and white, actually."

"Haven't been sleeping well lately," he said with a shrug. He let himself sag into a chair.

"What's on your mind? Anything we should talk about?"

Here was the moment, the tipping point; it was almost funny how they came so unexpectedly in life. Here was the moment when he should have said Yes, yes actually there is, then sat down and told his mother everything. But his mind was humming, clicking through the options, scanning the moves left to him. No problem was insurmountable—and certainly not this one. He had heard, for example, that there was serious poker in Minneapolis at the Canterbury Park pony track; it would take some driving, and he'd have to put up with actual people, cigar smoke and sunglasses. But with a steady, by-the-book, disciplined game—and hey, why not some luck?—he could get back in the black and nobody would be the wiser. And once he had done that, once he had paid off his and Gran's credit cards, he would be done with poker for good.

"I think I just need some sleep," he said.

"I'd certainly agree," his mother said. After his snack, he could feel her eyes on him as he mounted the stairs.

In bed he tried to sleep, but his mind played imaginary hands. One after another, he was on a streak, on a roll—nobody could touch him. He was that lucky, he was that good.

Will Weaver

Will Weaver's young adult novels include *Striking Out, Memory Boy, Claws, Full Service,* and *Defect* (2007). His short stories for young adults can be found in various anthologies, including *On the Fringe* and *No Easy Answers,* edited by Don Gallo. An avid outdoorsman, he lives on the upper Mississippi River near Bemidji, Minnesota. Growing up, he was not allowed to play cards. He now enjoys cards, but never for real money and never when he could be having fun with family and friends.

GLOSSARY

All-in—To go "all-in" is to bet all the money you have on the table.

Bad beat—When a good hand loses to a long-shot draw.

Blind—A forced bet that a player must make before the cards are dealt. In most holdem games there are two blind bets—the "small blind" and the "big blind." The big blind is usually double the amount of the small blind.

Board—The playing surface, usually a tabletop.

Boat—A full house. Also called a "full boat."

Bump—To raise.

Buy-in—The amount of chips a player must buy to sit in on a game.

Call—To match a bet.

Case card—The last available card of a rank. (If three aces are showing, only the "case ace" remains in the deck.)

Check—To decline an option to bet.

Check-raise—To check, then raise when your opponent bets.

Eight-or-better—A form of high-low in which the low hand must contain five unpaired cards eight or lower to qualify.

Flop—The first three up cards (community cards used by all active players) in a hand of holdem.

Fold—To drop out of a hand.

Gutshot—A draw to an inside straight.

Heads-up—A poker hand involving only two players.

Heater—A run of winning hands. Also called a "rush."

High-Low—Any poker game in which the high hand and the low hand split the pot.

Holdem—The most popular poker game in the world. Also called Texas holdem.

Hole cards—The cards dealt facedown to each player.

Light—In some games, when a player does not have enough chips to make a bet, he or she is allowed to "go light," or borrow money from the pot. If the player loses, he must repay the borrowed amount.

Limp in—To call an opening bet.

Omaha—A form of holdem in which each player receives four hole cards, and must use exactly two of them to make up a five-card hand. Omaha is most often played high-low.

Pocket pair—In holdem, when you have two hole cards of the same rank (i.e., two tens) you have a pocket pair.

Quads—Four-of-a-kind.

Rag—A low card that does not seem to help any of the players.

Raise—To bet more chips than the previous bettor.

River—The fifth and last up card in holdem.

Sandbag—To check-raise.

Set—Three-of-a-kind.

Suited—Two or more cards of the same suit.

Tell—A mannerism or action by which a player unintentionally reveals something about his hand.

Tilt—When a player begins to gamble wildly, calling and raising foolishly, he is said to be *on tilt*. Also called "steaming."

Trips—Three-of-a-kind.

Turn—The fourth up card in holdem.

Wired—A pocket pair: "I bet my *wired* kings."